ry of Congress Cataloging-in-Publication Data

z, 1948-
arah ran away with the veterinarian / Liz Newall.
    cm.
: 1-877946-45-1 : $22.00
way wives—United States—Fiction.
ily—United States—Fiction. 3. Women—United States—
n.   I. Title.
64.E558W49 1994   93-27524
.54—dc20   CIP

Manufactured in the United States of America

First Edition, November, 1994 -- 1,500 copies

THE PERMANENT PRESS
Noyac Road
Sag Harbor, NY 11963

WHY SA
RAN AWAY
THE VETERINA.

Libr

All rights re
thereof, in a

Newall, L
Why S
p.
ISBN
1. Run
2. Fa
Fictic
PS3
813

Liz Newall

THE PERMANENT PRESS
Sag Harbor, NY 11963

This book is dedicated to
Anna Dean and Curtis Pennington
for life and love

PART I

ANNIVERSARY

DONNA

This is the anniversary of what Daddy calls the most shameful day in the Crawford family history — the day my sister ran off with a veterinarian. Andrew says "recent" history. He's my husband. Not a Crawford by birth and not always sympathetic to Daddy's sense of pride. Andrew's from Massachusetts.

Getting back to Sarah, my sister, I think it had something to do with her reading *Lonesome Dove*. This is why. Sarah's vet was a horse specialist. In *Lonesome Dove* there were herds and herds of horses and rugged men, too, the kind that sleep in their boots and nothing else. It may have put her in the cowboy mood.

I say so too. Right at the Sunday dinner table. I expect Mama and Aunt Kate to agree. They both read the book. But they don't say anything. Nobody does. Daddy just keeps scraping across Mama's good china with his knife. Mama always uses her good china on Sunday. Daddy keeps scraping and scraping with that knife until finally Aunt Kate speaks up, "Bad Creek's playing down at the Wayfarer again. Heard them last night."

Then Mama lifts the rice bowl. "Rice is a little sticky today," she says, handing it to Daddy. But Daddy doesn't take it. He just sits there looking in his plate. Then he lays his knife down real slow and says, "A book don't make a woman just up and leave her husband! Or the rest of her family! Sarah read all the time growing up and she never did anything crazy before!"

Mama sets down the rice bowl and cuts her eyes at Daddy.

"Not that crazy," he says, a little lower. Then he takes the bowl and spoons out a wad of rice. Mama goes for more rolls and the rest of us let Sarah's anniversary rest in peace, at least at the dinner table.

But Andrew and I talk about it at home. He says maybe it was more "lonesome" than "dove," not that he's faulting Jack. None of us are. Jack's her husband. In twenty years of marriage he never did anything bad to Sarah, that we know of. Maybe her birthday had something to do with it. Andrew says turning forty is hard on a woman like Sarah, especially with no children. She's loved my two girls like her own but I don't guess it's the same.

I miss Sarah more than I'd miss Andrew, I think. I lived with her longer. Not that I'd run off and leave my husband, you understand. But since she's been gone I've had to do things by myself, things we used to do together. Like driving. Sarah always drove when we went anywhere together. Now I have to drive that old Honda. And I hate changing gears. Time you're in one, you have to get in another one. Then you come to a stop sign and you have to start all over. I've had to shop alone, which I hate to do, pick out Mama and Daddy's birthday gifts by myself, cook for Sunday dinner twice as often. And I haven't had anybody to really talk to, not about sister stuff — like what was happening on our programs and things about people we grew up with and how Mama and Daddy were getting along.

Andrew says I should get a job. To be honest, sometimes he gives more advice than I want. Not that I mind working. But he expects me to go to the library, dig through a bunch of heavy books, and do all this research on jobs of the future. He says, "Donna, you've got to become acquainted with the market." It's not like I'm planning a career. I already have one — taking care of him and the girls. I told him the only thing I wanted to get acquainted with is a new face now and then and a little mad money. He can't understand that. Sarah would.

Maybe I just need a make-over instead of a job, the kind you see in magazines, a little picture of what some woman really looks like and a big picture of the way she looks after a man with a pigtail or some other expert spends a few hours on her. When I have time, I flip through the new magazines at Bi-Lo looking for make-overs. Bi-Lo is a grocery story, pronounced "buy-low." The first time Andrew saw it he thought it was "be-low" which made me laugh, but then he's not from around here. But getting back to the make-overs, they always amaze me. I see the "before" and think, poor thing, she'd stop a clock. Then I see the "after" and quit feeling sorry for her real fast.

My favorite part is looking at "before" and figuring what I'd do if I were the expert. Like on this redhead with freckles and pale blue eyes. I would have told her, "Leave your hair straight, trimmed a little but not 'chemically altered,' add some eyeliner, and SMILE." That's one thing I learned from being Local Little Miss Sunbeam, that and how to tear bread so it splits right down the middle. It's harder than it looks. You've got to pinch the crust just right and tear fast. But as for the redhead, those New York experts permed her right up to her scalp, gave her "blond highlights" they called it, lined her lips, and turned her eyes green. I missed completely, except for the smile. She was smiling — that's half the make-over.

The "befores" usually look like they just had a tooth filled and the "afters" like they're headed for a date with Harrison Ford or some other hunk. Maybe the experts tell them something like, "Put on this yellow shirt and think of mud." "Now, put on this royal blue cashmere sweater and look like you think all this is free."

Still a make-over might be just what I need. Sarah never cared much about makeup, but I bet she'd tell me, "Go for it, Nonna!" She always called me "Nonna." Mama said she couldn't quite get the "D" right in Donna when she was little, but I think she called me Nonna to be different. God, I miss her.

Sarah's written a few times on motel stationery, a Travel Lodge in Raleigh, then a Howard Johnson's in Tennessee. Now her letters are postmarked Texas but they're still on motel stationery. Guess she stocked up while they were on the move. Don't know what they did with the horse. The letters don't really say much. Just that she's okay and something about the countryside, like dust storms in Lubbock are orange fog, and if you see a big tree in Amarillo, there's always a house underneath it. And there's more windmills out West than back home.

Jack still thinks she was kidnapped. I told him about the letters. He read a few but just flipped them back at me and said, "They don't prove a thing since she doesn't say anything about me. Maybe they're forged!"

"Maybe you don't know her all that well," I told him.

"I've lived with her longer than you have, Donna Jean!" He and Daddy are the only two in the family who call me Donna Jean and believe me they don't say it the same way. He turned his back on me after that, so I left.

I haven't talked to him since then. He doesn't eat Sunday dinner with the rest of us now. I hadn't even heard his name mentioned the last few months until I stopped at the Dixie store a week ago Friday. I go there for the chicken specials and ice cream. They have German chocolate crunch, low fat. Anyway, I talked to Joanne

[5

McJunkin who runs a cash register out there. She brought his name up.

Joanne said, "Donna, tell me about that brother-in-law of yours."

"I don't see him enough to tell one thing or the other."

Joanne rolled her eyes and lowered her voice. "I see him every week or so."

"What's he buy?" I asked, but I was watching her real close to make sure she didn't run my chicken across that little beeper twice. She's been known.

"Beer," Joanne said, "sometimes breakfast stuff and dog food, Jim Dandy I think, but always beer. He looks real bad, Donna, like he's had the flu or something." Joanne straightened her name tag which she always wears on the end of her left boob. "I speak to him, you know, try to cheer him up." She cleared her throat. "Is Sarah coming back any time soon?"

I didn't answer.

Then she said almost defiant-like, "A man like Jack needs a woman to look after him."

I shot right back, "He's got one. Now give me a freezer bag for that ice cream."

That's Joanne for you. A female vulture waiting to swoop down on what's not protected. She'd probably act the same way about my Andrew if I was to go on vacation too long without him. Of course, I never have. But if I did, there'd be ole Joanne in a tight red sweater and Ambush perfume hovering over Andrew to see what she could "do" for him. I wouldn't have anything to do with her except she's Aunt Lonita's second cousin. But she might be right about Jack. He prides himself on knowing things, being in control, and it breaks him up when he misses. Like with Sarah. Not knowing her like he thought he did. It probably did give him the flu.

But, growing up, you do things you might not tell your husband later. "Personality clues," Andrew calls them. Games for instance. Like when Sarah and I used to play stretch with Mama's ice pick. Sarah made it up. What you do is fling the ice pick so that it sticks in the ground. Then you keep one foot where you are and stretch the other one to the ice pick. The winner is the one who stretches the farthest without falling. I was always careful. I'd drop the ice pick where I knew I could reach it. But Sarah would flip it out so far she'd have to do a split to get there. She usually won except one morning when the grass was wet. She had me beat but when she pulled up the ice pick, she slipped sideways and slammed it right into her thigh. I can still see it — the handle looked glued to her skin. She turned white and blank. Then she told me quietlike, "Pull it out, Nonna. Pull it out." I couldn't. I wanted to but I just couldn't.

I ran for Mama and she came out screaming, "ICE PICK!" like it was the single most horrible object in the human existence. By then Sarah had jerked it out and was lying back on the grass, one narrow stream of blood easing across her thigh. Mama sent me inside for iodine and a towel. She wiped off the blood and poured the whole bottle on that tiny red circle. Mama took Sarah to Dr. Sams and got a tetanus shot. Sarah's arm swelled up, her leg stayed browny-orange for about a week, and a wide circle rose up around the ice-pick hole. Dr. Sams said that's because the pick went in so far. Mama stayed mad about as long as the iodine stain lasted. Looking back, I guess she was worried but it seemed more like something else was bothering her. I can still hear her wailing "ICE PICK!"

I never heard her use that tone of voice but one other time and that was with Sarah too. This time it was "RODEO!" It was the summer after Sarah graduated from high school. She was working at the Dixie store when the Southern Circuit Rodeo came to town. It was a first-rate rodeo, not the amateur kind the fire department used to put on once a year with donkey ball and cow plops. It lasted three days but the riders came in a few days early to settle in. Most of them made a trip to the Dixie store and stocked up for the week. But this one rodeo rider, he kept coming back and coming back, two or three times a day. And he always went through Sarah's checkout line.

All she could talk about was Johnny. I can hear her like it was yesterday. She said, "Nonna, he looks just like Little Joe." And after that we'd go around the house humming the theme to "Bonanza."

We went to all three nights of the rodeo. Sarah and I sat off by ourselves as close to the arena railing as we could and rated the cowboys. Three points for good riding, three for good-looking, and a bonus point if we liked their boots and minus a point if we saw them spit.

"Look at that one!" Sarah said, pointing at a cowboy balancing on the arena fence. He had on a red shirt, black hat, and tight, tight jeans.

"I can't see his face for his hat."

"I can," Sarah said, wiggling the whole bench.

"He's got a mustache," I whispered, caught up in Sarah's wiggle.

"I wonder," Sarah said, running her fingers across her lips, "if it tickles when he kisses."

"I hope he doesn't spit!"

We broke in to semi-hysterics and I was so glad Mama and Daddy weren't nearby to hear us.

Every time it was Johnny's turn, Sarah would get real quiet, hold her breath, and squeeze my wrist, like somehow the both of us could pull him through. As soon as his ride was over, Sarah would kind of yelp and shake the whole bench again.

In between rodeo nights, Johnny kept coming through Sarah's checkout line. By the end of the third night, Sarah was in love. Johnny talked her into leaving with him for Charlotte the next day. It was all so romantic that I was wishing I had somebody to run away with too. When you're fifteen even sawdust seems romantic. But I should have known how upset Mama and Daddy would be, with Sarah all set to enter college in the fall.

I guess Sarah and I both acted a little giddy the day she was to leave, humming that "Bonanza" tune, because Mama figured something was going on. As soon as Sarah went to work, Mama grilled me and I told. Just like that. Somehow I thought she'd be impressed with the romance of it all. But she grew as pale as Sarah had with the ice pick in her leg. And she wailed in that Godawful ice-pick voice, "RODEO!" Then she told Daddy. Daddy headed straight for the rodeo camp and I still don't know what he said or did, but by the time Sarah left work Johnny was gone.

She kept to herself the rest of the summer, mostly reading when she wasn't working, but by the time college started she seemed over the rodeo thing. And she didn't even seem to hold it against me for telling. But we never talked about the rodeo again.

When Sarah started college, Daddy said it was like she "gained a new lease on life." Aunt Kate said, "more likely, it was something she lost that had her smiling." Either way she was a whole lot happier. The main source — Jack Brighton. The rest of us met Jack at Sunday dinner. Mama was having baked ham and Daddy cut it like he always did, putting some crusty outside slices to one side for me. But Jack found them first, and forked up all three pieces. We were all sitting there eating except Mama, who was up and down seeing about more rolls, more ice, the usual, when Daddy casually started asking questions.

Daddy said, "Jack, what're you majoring in?"

"Majoring in business, minoring in Sarah," he said without batting an eye. Then he cut his eyes at Sarah and said, "Or is it the other way around?" Sarah blushed and giggled.

Daddy looked like he forgot what he was going to say. Jack went straight into talking about marketing and consumer index. I think he was trying to impress Daddy but Daddy couldn't keep up. I tell you, I thought Jack had cut his own throat with a dinner knife. But then Daddy coughed a couple of times and said, "I'm in the market myself for a pick-up truck."

"New or used?" Jack said, laying down his fork.

"Broke in good," Daddy said.

"Anything to trade in?" Jack asked.

"My old Chevy," Daddy said, wiping his mouth.

"Condition?"

"Fair."

"Tires?"

"Four round ones."

And on they went until Jack had narrowed the field to a few dealerships and they set a date to go truck hunting. Then Jack finished off with two pieces of Mama's peach pie. And in one Sunday dinner Jack had the whole family sliced, wrapped, and ready to go. Everybody but me. Aunt Kate wouldn't have fallen for it either if she'd been there. But she was off hiking with her new boyfriend.

Jack was already a junior in college and as soon as he graduated he and Sarah got married. Mama wanted the ceremony at Beulah Land Baptist Church, where I got married later, but Sarah insisted on it being outside in Aunt Kate's pasture. There was a real pretty spot near an old tenant shack. Sarah said, "I want it right by the old house, Mama. It'll be so romantic!" Mama got that ice-pick look. Sarah and I thought it was kind of strange, but Mama didn't explain or stop Sarah from having it there. Aunt Kate had to keep the horses off the lot for a week and it took that long for Daddy and Jack and Aunt Kate's boyfriend at the time, not the hiking one, to clear out the horse biscuits. They got most of them.

On the day of the wedding, buttercups and little white daisies were in bloom all over the place. Sarah wore Mama's wedding dress. It was so pretty, maybe just a little yellow up real close, but

[9

Sarah wanted to wear it no matter what. It had mutton sleeves that looked like something out of old England and lace that went clear up to Sarah's chin.

Sarah made the wedding cake herself. It was flat and shaped like a heart. The inside was pink and tasted sort of like strawberries. She made it from a mix but everybody said they couldn't tell. The wedding went well until the end when Aunt Kate decided to throw oats instead of rice. Daddy said, "These must be Kate's wild oats." Kate said something back which I didn't hear. Daddy turned red but he was laughing.

We all started scooping double handfuls out of this huge burlap bag and throwing oats like crazy. We caught Sarah and Jack coming through the gate. They were laughing and throwing up their hands. At least Sarah was laughing. Jack kept covering his face and making funny noises so we really bombed him. Then he started running. But we had him surrounded — me and Kate on one side and Daddy and even Mama on the other. Finally he stopped running and just stood there wheezing and sniffling and rubbing his eyes. That's when we found out Jack was allergic to oats. Still is, I guess. His eyes turned puffy red and he was sneezing so hard he could barely feed Sarah cake for the wedding picture. But he didn't complain or get mad or anything. At least he didn't say so. By the time they left for the honeymoon, he was better and everyone agreed they made a nice couple riding away.

When they got back, they seemed real happy. They'd laugh and cut their eyes at each other sort of in secret signals even at Sunday dinner with Mama and Daddy watching. And you could tell they were rubbing each other under the table. It got to be a little annoying, not that I was jealous or anything. It's just that I'd always been what Aunt Kate called, "Sarah's chief confidant and giggle partner." Now Jack was. I knew love was supposed to be that way and it's not that I didn't like Jack. I just missed Sarah so much, even though she was still here.

That was before I met Andrew. The first thing he ever said to me was, "I'm Andrew and you're Beautiful." He sounded just like one of the Kennedys, his accent and all. We were in the college auditorium and I'll never forget. We had to sneak around at first to date, him being an instructor and me being a freshman. But I finally brought him home to meet everybody at Sunday dinner. I was nervous but he acted real calm. He taught psychology, still does, so he knew how to calm himself. Everybody was there.

Mama, Daddy, Sarah, Jack, and even Aunt Kate. She was between boyfriends. We could always tell because she'd show up for Sunday dinner saturated in Virginia Slims and acting real restless, "like a worm in ashes," Daddy would say. Mama had fried chicken. That was when it was still okay to fry things. I remember it was chicken because somebody said "You are what you eat." Then Aunt Kate said, "Maybe that's why I feel mad as an old wet hen." Not even Daddy would mess with Kate in a mood like that but Andrew didn't know.

He spoke up and said, "It's been scientifically proven that wet hens don't exhibit temper." I don't know if it was his accent or what he said but Kate's mouth fell open. I was just glad she wasn't chewing. Andrew didn't seem to notice. I guess he thought he was impressing the family because everybody was staring at him. He took a sip of tea and said, "Kate," which seemed kind of familiar just having met her, "do you mean 'mad' as in 'angry' or 'mad' as in 'crazy'? If it's crazy, then you may be right. A wet hen might show psychotic tendencies. I don't think there's been a study on that." He pushed his sweater sleeves up a notch like he'd made a point.

Kate leaned forward and said, "What I mean is I'm mad as hell, pissed off, fucking angry!" Andrew reared back like he'd been singed. Mama jumped up to get more tea. Sarah and Jack quit rubbing each other under the table. Daddy looked like he might laugh. I thought for sure Kate would leave the table, but she sat right there gnawing her chicken down to the pully bone.

I just wanted to die, but after dinner things got a little better. Kate went home to smoke, Sarah and Jack went home to finish what they started under the table, and Daddy and Andrew went in the living room to talk. I stayed in the kitchen with Mama. When Andrew left he thanked Mama for dinner and Daddy for all the gardening tidbits — "tidbits" was Andrew's word — and he left. I didn't see him for about a month after that, and I got to wondering if I ever would again.

But he showed up pretty soon all love sick, saying, "Donna, I can't live without you even if . . . even if . . ." He never did say "even if" what. We got married at Beulah Land. It was a pretty wedding. I can see the front pew now. Mama was sitting there in ice-blue chiffon kind of dazed-like, tired I guess, but Daddy was crying. He was slumped over, trying to hide it, but I could tell. Heck, everybody could. His shoulders were heaving and he'd let out a snort ever so often. At first it looked like he was snoring or laughing. But he looked up once and his face was as wet as Jack's had been the day we pelted him with oats. Sarah was crying too. She was my matron of honor. She had on a long blue gown, about two shades deeper than Mama's but they didn't clash or anything. It had a full skirt and tiny waist and short puffy sleeves like Cinderella's ball gown. She kept saying stuff like, "Oh, Nonna, you're so pretty!" and "Oh, Nonna, are you sure he's it?" She cried too. Not many of Andrew's relatives came, being so far and all, but he didn't care and neither did I. It's funny how you get kind of selfish when you're in love. You know other people are caring about you but all you can think about is each other. It was a nice wedding.

About the time I got married, Sarah and Jack started trying to have babies. They tried for a long time but Sarah kept miscarrying, one after the other. It seemed like every year she'd get pregnant and a few months later she'd miscarry. She kept getting thinner and thinner. Dr. Sams, he was our family doctor, he finally told her and Jack not to try anymore, another miscarriage could kill her. But Sarah kept on. She tricked Jack into two more pregnancies before he wised up and got a vasectomy. We're not supposed to know about the vasectomy but Sarah told me and I told Andrew. That was four years ago. Or five, I guess, counting the year she's been gone.

What I can't understand is why Sarah didn't tell me she was taking off. I mean, good Lord, I'm her sister! She did mention the vet a time or two. Michael was his name. "Nonna," she said, "you should see his eyes. They're dark as night." But the few times I saw him, he was wearing a cowboy hat pulled down so low I couldn't even tell if he had eyes, much less what color they were. I guess Sarah got a lot closer. But she never said anything about leaving, not to me. That's what hurts. That and missing her so much.

JACK

It's not like I didn't love her or take care of her. Twenty years of paying Duke Power bills, good God, that ought to count for something.

Tommy told me I'd been warned. He told me the first time I brought Sarah home, she had the same look as my mother. I couldn't even remember my mother's face, but Tommy said, "Cat eyes. Watch out." Just before Sarah left, her eyes kept reminding me of something way back in my brain, maybe it was my mother. Guess that's what attracted me to her in the first place. Those green eyes, like marbles. And a mass of auburn hair. Sarah wore it longish and pulled back with one of those ponytail bands. But when she took the band off, her hair would leap out like a wild animal. The first time I saw her hair fly out like that, I wanted to grab it all up in my hands and just hold on to it. Andrew would probably call that primitive instinct. Maybe so. But I miss her hair, smelling like wild flowers, soft against my chest.

The things we've been through in twenty years. Like starting out at Mimosa Trailer Park. I was a rookie salesman at Jimmy Whittaker's Auto-Rama then. I got the customers nobody else wanted. The tire kickers, the be-backers, the half deaf, the *Consumer Guide* experts. The boys would say, "Go get 'em, Jack!" and I'd know I had a challenge on my hands. That's when we were living at Mimosa, Trailer #17. God, I hate mimosa trees. There were five of them. Sarah thought they were pretty with that little pink, puffy stuff that blew all over everything. Trash trees. That's what they are to most everybody except a few Southern romantics. What I hated was the way they messed up my car. I was driving a Karman Ghia at the time. Nothing expensive but it looked classy. Except with that pink crap plastered all over it. No matter where I parked, that stuff would get on it. I'd have to cover up the car every night or wash it off every morning when those mimosas were in heat.

But Sarah liked it there. Women are supposed to hate living in trailers. Not Sarah. Said it made her "feel like a gypsy." She liked the people too. Most of our neighbors were either young couples — some married, some shacked up — or old retired folks. I remember one couple, Judy and Roy, I never did get their last names. They weren't married. The girl worked for the Outside Inn and she always wore a tight red sweater and a short little black skirt, the kind you keep hoping they'll bend over in. I guess she wore something different on the weekends or on her day off but I didn't see her much then. Roy thought he was Super Salesman. He was always pushing something — World Book, club aluminum, knives.

One time he demonstrated this cutlery set for Sarah and me. Some steak knives, a butcher knife, a paring knife, an ice pick, a pair of super-duper scissors. We couldn't afford them but he said he got credit just for showing us. Sarah said she didn't much like looking at "all those weapons," but she kept stroking the handles, touching the blades, pressing her fingers against the points until one of them drew blood. She tried to hide it, but I saw her flinch, saw the blood pool up. Roy apologized for them being so sharp, but you could tell he thought it was a selling point. Then he took two quarters and cut them almost in half with the super-duper scissors. He bent them out like butterflies and stuck a little hole in each quarter with the ice pick. Sarah ran wire through the hole and made earrings. Those were her favorite for I don't know how long. But everytime she wore them, in my mind I could see her fingers dripping red. I can't remember when she stopped wearing them. Last I heard Roy was selling Amway, and Judy was selling real estate. Sarah still writes Judy, or did. Don't know if they ever got married.

Sarah did her best to fix up the inside of Unit #17. We had this tiny bedroom with a double bed that touched three walls. Sarah always slept by the window so she could see out. One night I came home, and there she was — barefooted, jeans, India blouse that never looked ironed, all wrapped up in a rainbow. She'd gotten this huge rainbow poster from the Dixie store — she was still working there at the time — some fruit punch advertisement, no, 7UP ad, I think. She cut out the rainbow and was about to glue it to the wall, the one at the foot of the bed. I helped her and it really looked nice, but I asked her why she didn't put it on the opposite wall, above the bedstead. That seemed the logical place to me.

"I thought about that, it hanging over our heads," she said, "but I'd rather see it when I wake up." She back-flopped onto the bed and rested her feet against the wall. "Now, I can touch it with my toes!" I jumped on top of her and we dedicated the new rainbow then and there.

We stayed at Mimosa two years. Guess the rainbow is still in Unit #17 if the trailer's standing. Sarah wanted to take it with us

Copyright © 1994 by Liz Newall.

Newall, Liz, 1948-
  Why Sarah ran away with the veterinarian / Liz Newall.
    p. cm.
  ISBN: 1-877946-45-1 : $22.00
1. Runaway wives—United States—Fiction.
2. Family—United States—Fiction. 3. Women—United States—
Fiction. I. Title.
PS3564.E558W49 1994   93-27524
813'.54—dc20   CIP

WHY SARAH RAN AWAY WITH THE VETERINARIAN

but she couldn't get it off the wall without ripping it. She did tear one end a little, but glued it back. "I'll have to leave it for the next couple," she said, "so they can touch the rainbow when they make love."

I learned a lot those first two years at Whittaker's. I read every bit of literature that came out — motors, wheelbase, structural advantages on each model. I'd always thumbed through *Consumer Report* and *Consumer Guide*, but I started studying them until I could out quote customers who came in with the latest issue. I could even tell them which loafbread they ought to be eating. It paid off. I got return customers. They'd be back to trade before their twenty-four months finance was up. These days, return customers tend to wait longer, three or four years. But back then, I had buyers like Dr. Sams. He'd trade in his Cadillac as soon as the new-car smell wore off.

I earned enough to get us out of the trailer and into an apartment complex, a town house. The guy who owned the place was a friend of Kate's, probably more than a friend. He offered us half rent if Sarah would collect the other tenants' rent and field their complaints, call the plumber, stuff like that. Sarah jumped at the chance. She got to meet all the tenants and she was really good at handling complaints. Except for one, I remember. Pairs of apartments were like mirrors so the bedrooms butted up against each other and the dividing wall was cracker thin. The bedrooms were practically touching. The couple in #21 enjoyed romping around and shouting obscenities at each other while they made love. The couple in #22, however, didn't quite see it as a turn-on and beat on the wall the whole time. They both called Sarah and complained about each other. Sarah mentioned it to Donna. Donna told Andrew. At the very next Sunday dinner he spoke up.

"Sarah," he said, "Donna tells me you're having trouble with two couples at your apartments," he touched his collar, "over sexual expression."

Donna looked down fast and started rounding up her English peas. Sarah turned her head toward Andrew and kind of shook it. But Andrew didn't seem to notice.

"Everyone has a right," he said, reaching across Donna Jean for the rolls, "to sexual arousal by preference."

All the women turned beet red, except for Kate. Finally, Joe spoke up, "Lonita and Thomas just got back from Disney World."

"Had a wonderful time," Mrs. Crawford chimed in, "Lonita said the ride with dolls and boats was her favorite. She said 'It's a Little World.' "

"It's a Small World," Andrew said.

"Ain't it though," Mr. Crawford said, "but Thomas said Sea World was better."

Andrew rolled his eyes and went on, "My point is, it's harmful to restrict one's method of coupling, whether it's shouting obscenities or banging on the wall. It kills creativity."

Mrs. Crawford jumped up, mumbled something about dessert, and shot toward the kitchen.

"Vivienne, we don't need no pie yet," Mr. Crawford said, not looking up.

Mrs. Crawford slammed it on the table. "It's here in case anybody gets finished fast," she called over her shoulder and headed back into the kitchen.

"For God's sake!" Kate said, reaching for the pie, "just buy them some earplugs! Vivienne, got any ice cream to go on this pie?"

Times at the apartment and even at Mimosa were mostly good. Until the babies. But that was after we moved into a house over on Oak Street. Sarah was working for Dr. Sams by then. Front office stuff — keeping the books, making appointments, telling people they'd have to wait. It didn't pay that well but we got our medical care free. Which was good considering the problems Sarah had with the babies.

I know it was worse for her, at least the miscarrying part, but they were my babies too, and I cried after each one, not where she could see me but she knew. The first one about scared us both to death. Sarah didn't just come right out and tell me she was pregnant that first time. What she did was put this little blue rattler in my lunch. When I opened up the bag, there it was, no note or anything, just that little rattler. At first I thought I had the wrong lunch but everything else looked like the usual, a ham and mustard sandwich, a little bag of chips, a cookie, a paper napkin with XXX inked in one corner.

I was still holding the rattler when the phone rang. "How's your lunch, Jack?" she said and burst into giggles. It hit me like a new Mercedes. "You're pregnant!" I shouted. I dropped the receiver, ran through the showroom yelling, "She's pregnant!" and drove straight home to hold her. That was Sarah. She could never come right out and tell you something. She had to make it dramatic or mysterious.

She wasn't much over three months when she lost the first one. We'd already told all the Crawfords and my father, Tommy, too. Sarah had asked Dr. Sams if sex was okay and he said I probably couldn't shake the baby loose with a stick of dynamite. I remember that's what he said because I liked the comparison. Sarah said being pregnant made her feel sexy so we kept making love like always. But the night she miscarried, she said it didn't feel right. I quit right then. But it was too late. She rolled away from me, pulled her knees up tight against her abdomen, and started crying, "It hurts, Jack! It hurts so bad!" I slipped up close behind her and put my arms around her. That's when I felt the blood, cold and wet, covering my thighs. I threw back the sheet and saw a red pool, growing each time she cried out. I wrapped her in the bed spread and took her straight to the hospital. But they couldn't do anything.

Dr. Sams came by the next day. He said it was nature's way of getting rid of defects — those were his words — and we were probably lucky. I'm no psychology expert like Andrew, but even I know that's not the thing to tell a grieving woman. Whether it's true or not. I told Sarah I was going for some coffee. Then I went out in the hall, put my face against the concrete wall, and cried like I was six years old again. When I came back, she looked like her mind was somewhere else but I could tell she'd been crying too. We never cried together.

That was the first one and probably the hardest I guess. After that we knew what to expect. Sarah would put old sheets on the bed as soon as she found out she was pregnant. I never looked for a rattler in my lunch again, just old sheets. That and no sex. One time she went six months. Now that I think about it, I guess that one was the hardest to take. After that, I didn't want to try again. But Sarah would beg. "I'll make it to seven months next time," she'd say. I can't remember how many she lost after that. I'm good with numbers, but I kind of lost track.

I finally went under the knife and put a stop to it. Lovemaking wasn't much for a while. Sarah was willing enough, just not eager. Any man knows the difference, but I got by. That was years ago, five to be exact. If that was why she left, she'd have taken off five years ago, wouldn't she?

Maybe a regular doctor wouldn't be so hard to take or an actor like when the Carradine brothers were filming a movie over in

Clayton. Or a good-looking jeweler, if there is such a thing. He could have lured her away with rings and bracelets. Sarah loved opals and gold loops and etched-out pins. But a horse doctor! I can't make sense of it.

What really gets me is the way she was in bed with me those last weeks. Every night if I wanted. She acted like she did twenty years ago when we couldn't get enough of each other. Just the same. That's why I still think that horse doctor may have doped her. That's the only way she'd have left me. You hear about horse tranquilizers all the time. Hell, he may still be drugging her and that's why she hasn't come home. Or maybe he's got her addicted and she's physically dependent on the bastard. I know that's only a slim chance, about a two-to-four percent chance, but I can't blame her completely. At least not hate her. I mean, how would you feel if you hated someone for a whole year and then found out they'd been drugged?

Another thing. Sarah loved to write letters. Cousins, friends, people from the Mimosa days, she'd send them these long letters telling them I'd earned us a trip to Hawaii at the car lot or that I'd made a big sale like the July 4th Sell-a-thon. Sometimes she'd have me sign the letters. And she'd write me notes and put them in my lunch bag, back when I was still taking my lunch. One time she put a note in my sandwich, right between the ham and cheese, and I ate it. It was little, I guess, and I never saw it, or tasted it either. Don't know what it said. Maybe she was kidding when she told me I ate it. She'd say things like that sometimes. I never knew for sure. But the point is, if she was leaving she would have written me a letter telling me where she was going and why. Then she would have signed it XXX. Other people just don't know her like I do. That's why I still think she may have been drugged and kidnapped or wifenapped, if there is such a word.

I hired a detective. The Crawfords don't know that. They just gave up right away, but not me. Took him a week to find her, $100 a day plus travel expenses. Then he watched her another three days, his meter still running. And you know what he told me? Said Sarah looked "quite comfortable" and "there of her own voli- tion." Fuck volition! I started not to pay him. I know her better than some stranger who watches her three days. I know her better than her own sister for that matter. Donna Jean showed me some letters Sarah might have written but that doesn't mean he didn't make her say things. If she'd had her "own volition" she'd have left me a letter. I know.

Of course, there's a chance that the letter got lost. I've torn up the house looking for it. The kitchen, anyway. She always left stuff like that on the refrigerator under one of those little fruit magnets. We have six. I even moved the refrigerator out from the wall — a Whirlpool, fourteen years old and still running — took off the front vent and vacuumed the coils and all under it. It was a mess, too. Looked like a couple of furry animals had gotten under there and died. A bunch of dust, I tell you. Guess Sarah hadn't cleaned it out in a while. That's not like her. She's so neat she even washes out the dog's bowl before she feeds him. Says he's our only child.

Bilo, that's our dog, came riding up with Sarah about three years ago. Four years now that she's been gone. She went out for groceries at Bi-Lo and came back with a dog. She said he was running around the parking lot about to get run over. She had the bag boy load him with the rest of the stuff. And that's the way I first saw him, wedged between a bag of charcoal and a jug of Clorox. This little two-toned dog, yellow and brown, not much to look at. But Sarah wanted to keep him so I gave in.

Bilo was already grown. The veterinarian, a small-animal vet not a wife-stealing horse jerk, said Bilo was about four years old and had probably roamed most of his life. Sarah used to say she wished he could talk so he could tell her where he'd been. The funny thing is, the last few weeks I'd hear her saying things like, "Do you miss roaming, Puppy?" or "Bilo, what's out there?" Or sometimes she'd whisper stuff to him that I couldn't hear. I can't see Sarah leaving Bilo. She was crazy about the dog. I guess that vet didn't mess with small animals, just horses and other men's wives.

Maybe I should have noticed about her talking to Bilo, but everybody talks to their dog, don't they? I even talk to Bilo now. Who else do I have? At first Donna Jean kept asking me did I notice Sarah doing anything strange before she disappeared. I told her not anything stranger than usual. I mean the whole Crawford clan is wired a little loosely, some more than a little.

I haven't seen any of them except Donna Jean since this thing with Sarah happened. Last time I was over there was for Sunday dinner. Joe was talking about special powers people who were close to nature had, like himself.

"What's your sixth sense?" Andrew asked, opening his napkin.

"It's not a sixth sense," Joe said, "it's one of my five." He reached for the corn. "Grew it myself."

"So what is it?" Andrew asked.

"Corn, Silver Queen variety," Joe said, reaching for the butter.

"I mean the extra power," Andrew said. He was starting to fidget like he always does when he talks to Joe over two minutes.

"Snakes," Joe said. He cut a pat of butter and rubbed it against the corn.

"What about snakes?"

"I already buttered the corn," Vivienne said, frowning at Joe. She looked at Andrew. "Joe can smell snakes."

"Smell snakes?" Andrew's brows shot up and his napkin slipped off his lap.

Joe nodded.

"Where do you go to smell snakes?" Andrew reached for his napkin, not taking his eyes off Joe.

"The garden."

"How do they smell?"

"Musty, damp. Kind of like old bread," Joe said, rolling his corn against shrinking butter. "That's how black snakes smell. Rat snakes smell dryer."

I wasn't sure if Joe was serious or if he was just having fun with Andrew, but either way he had Andrew going. I glanced at Sarah, but she was staring across the table. I squeezed her thigh. Nothing.

Donna Jean spoke up. "Daddy's cousin is a fire witch."

"A what?" Andrew said, a hint of irritation.

"Fire witch," Donna said, "you know, talks out burns."

Joe chewed a bite of corn, then wiped his chin. "Don't y'all have any witches in Massachusetts?" he said. "I thought that's where they got started."

Andrew didn't answer.

"Some people can talk off warts, some can talk out burns. It's a God-given power."

"It's superstition," Andrew said, louder than necessary. Donna patted him on the arm. "The thing is," he said, a little lower, "you hear these stories second or third hand, but you never actually meet someone who's experienced this miraculous healing." He reached for an ear of corn.

"I have," Joe said.

"Met somebody who experienced this special power?"

"No," Joe said, "experienced it myself." He laid his corn down. "I fell on a wood stove in grade school. It was a real cold day and Miss Drake, she was our teacher, she had that stove popping hot. I tripped over a stick of wood. My chin landed on top of the stove and commenced to frying like an egg. My hands stuck to the sides.''

Donna and Vivienne shuddered. Kate split a roll. Sarah stared into space.

"Andrew, you haven't touched a bite of dinner," Vivienne said. "Let me heat it up for you." She reached for his plate.

"It's fine," he said, holding on tight, "just fine." He took a bite of corn. "Go on, Joe," he said between chews.

"I left skin on that stove everywhere I touched it. I can still smell it. Miss Drake ran home with me then and there. It was only a mile or so. Mama said she heard me yelling before she saw me. When she found out what happened, she rushed me over to cousin Zooney's. She was my Mama's first cousin. What does that make her to me?''

"Second, I think," Kate said.

"Or third," Donna said.

"No," said Vivienne, "it's first cousin once removed."

"Get on with it!" Andrew shouted. Donna cleared her throat.

"I went into cousin Zooney's sitting room, still screaming. She ran Mama out, sat me down, and took both my hands in hers. Then she started chanting-like.''

"Singing?" Kate asked.

"Not exactly. More sing-songy talking."

"What were the words?" Donna asked.

Joe tilted his head. "To be honest, Donna Jean, I don't remember. I heard her but I think her powers wiped it from my memory. Anyway . . .''

"Like those people who get examined by space aliens?" Donna Jean asked.

Andrew shot a look at Donna Jean. "Anyway?" he said. You could tell he was grinding his teeth.

Joe looked down at the corn. "Anyway, she talked the fire right out. It quit hurting and when Mama came back in the room she said I was playing patty-cake with cousin Zooney." Joe picked up the corn, took a bite, and smiled while he chewed.

"Mind over matter," Andrew said. "It's simple psychology. She got your mind off the pain with a silly song and a little game." His eyes swept the table. "But," he said, "she couldn't make the burns disappear!''

Joe laid down the corn and held both palms up. He stuck his chin out so we could see underneath it. "Then why don't I have any scars?" he asked. Andrew gave up.

I wanted to laugh. But I thought I'd hold it until Sarah and I were alone. "Was that fire-witch story true?" I asked her driving home.

"What?"

"That story your father told."

"I didn't hear it," she said. She was staring out the window. That's all she said, so I just let it drop.

When I think about it, there were other times she acted different, too. When I think about it! Hell, I've thought about it for the past 365 days! Sarah must have locked her keys in the Cutlass a dozen times last year. But I never said anything about it, not mean anyway. I just sent over Chip, he's our rookie salesman, with a spare. And sometimes Sarah stayed up half the night reading some book, but she never seemed to finish one. She'd have three or four novels around the house opened face down like spraddled-out A's. If I asked her what she was reading she'd say something different every time.

Then the horse business. It was right before Sarah's fortieth birthday. She'd been acting different, like I said. I figured it was her birthday coming on. I hardly remember my fortieth, things were so busy at the lot. We'd just got the go-ahead to do a promo on a bunch of mini-vans. Men just aren't affected the same. At least I wasn't. Steve Brock, he's my best salesman when he's not trying to impress the lastest office temp, anyway, Steve was telling me one morning what happened when his wife hit 40. "She quit her job at the bank," he said, "didn't ask me or anything." He filled his mug. "Then," he said, embarrassed-like, "she dug out her high school charm bracelet, strapped the thing on, and signed up for cosmetology school." Steve couldn't make eye contact. Disaster for a salesman.

Cid, he's head of service, heard Steve. Cid parts his hair over his left ear and swoops it over. Looks like hell on a windy day. "You got off easy," he said, fingering the Krispie Kremes. "My wife had liposuction, bought a new wardrobe, and traded in our mini-van for a '65 Mustang." He licked his fingers and chose a doughnut.

"Where?" Steve and I asked at the same time.

Cid didn't look up. "Her thighs."

"No," I said, "where'd she get the Mustang?"

"Karl's Used Car Corral," he whispered.

Nobody said anything for a minute. I filled my cup, took a pull, and said with more confidence than I was feeling, "Sarah's not like that."

"Just wait until the big 4-0." Steve said, pulling at his gold rope necklace. Cid nodded and swept his hand across his hair, left to right.

But I got busy and didn't think about the birthday thing again until a month or so later. I came home one evening and there Sarah was sitting cross-legged in the den. She looked up and smiled like I hadn't seen in months or maybe years. "Guess what I want for my birthday, Jack?" she said, her knees pumping up and down.

"What birthday?" I said, remembering the conversation at the coffee pot.

"You know! So guess."

"A diamond? New underwear? I know — leather boots, a whip, and one of those cute little garter belts?"

"No, no, and NOOOOOOO!" She quit bobbing her knees. She opened her eyes wide and took a deep breath, for dramatic effect I knew.

"A horse!"

"What's wrong with the Cutlass?"

"To ride, not drive!" And before I could say anymore, she pulled me down beside her and started reading horse-for-sale ads. I didn't really listen. I was too busy watching her excitement and thinking how eager she'd be in bed. She was my Sarah again. And I figured the horse thing was like the high school charm bracelet, something to ease in forty. I couldn't say no.

Sarah found the horse she wanted and I got the owner down from $800 to $500 plus a new truck liner. The liner was probably worth more than that nag. I hated to let him get me like that, but Sarah had her heart set and she'd already arranged to keep the horse at Kate's farm. I don't have a whole lot of use for Kate but I figured what trouble could Sarah get into at her aunt's farm taking care of a horse, for godsake. And Sarah did seem happier for a while. That is until the damn nag went lame. I'd have helped her myself if I knew anything about horses and if the stuff they feed horses didn't bother me so much. I told her to call an expert. Some expert! I still wonder if Kate had a hand in it.

They took the horse with them. Or that guy stole it. I think I would have shot it, taken a gun then shot it between the eyes if they'd left it. This whole thing has made me think like a raving lunatic. Maybe I'd have just sold it by the pound for dog food. Or fed it to Bilo.

SARAH

It has nothing to do with Jack. How can you fault the perfect husband? Smart, successful, still hot for me after twenty years. At least he was when I left. My leaving came from something else. For a whole year I heard it, faint at first like a song I'd forgotten, a dream without dialogue. It doesn't have that much to do with Michael either — except for those tan arms, hard as fence posts, eyes dark as a forest, the smell of leather — all in a cool, woodsy barn. Maybe it does have something to do with Michael. But I didn't meet him until the last month. By then, I'd been leaving in my mind almost a year.

It started about the time Dr. Sams retired. I thought at first I just missed the clinic, the regular hours, talking to Robbie Jo. She was the permanent nurse. Dr. Sams had others that came and went, but Robbie Jo had been there longer than me. She was blond and pretty except for her eyebrows. They looked a little strange like she'd tried to move them up a notch. The work-comp guys who came in from the mill loved her. She'd say, "Jimmy, come on back here with me," or "Charlie, tell me about that bruise," in a voice that hinted more than just checking temperature and blood-pressure.

On days when Dr. Sams was out, we kept the office open for book work and allergy shots. Robbie Jo and I would usually run across the street to the Quik Mart, buy some junk food, hide out in the back office, and talk.

One time I asked Robbie Jo about her husband.

"Which one?" she said, peeling the cellophane off a honey bun.

"Either one," I said.

"There's three. Take your pick." She bit into the top gooey layer.

"Husband number one."

"Harold," she said, chewing on one side. "He's dead. I thought love was forever but not when you cross a TV antenna and a power line." She swallowed. "It about killed me too. I was just a teenager." She looked at a Pharm-all calendar hanging on the opposite wall. "Funny thing is, I can hardly remember his face. I have some pictures but they don't seem real anymore." She took a smaller bite.

"Number two?" I said.

"I remember him all right." She smiled, distant like Aunt Kate does sometime. "Sam. Samuel Lee Pettimore. He killed a man." She wiped the sticky from her lip. "Lordy, lordy. He had a temper. But he was fun, Sarah. We had a ball. Every weekend we'd go riding on his Harley, not with a gang or anything, just him and me. I loved him like crazy." She took a long drink of Coke and wiped her lip again. She lowered her voice, "He's the kind of man that makes you want to kiss his thighs. Know what I mean, Sarah?"

I nodded. But I'd never kissed Jack's thighs, not even thought about it. I tried to picture it in my mind.

"But he killed a man," Robbie Jo said. "Knocked him down with a tire iron and didn't let him up until the coroner came."

My mind skipped from Jack's thighs to bloody asphalt.

"That's what they said. I wasn't with him at the time. I was spinning out laundry at Suds and Duds. Sam had been with me and I guess had too many suds. He left for a while. Never did come back. Still don't know what started the fight." Robbie Jo peeled more cellophane but she quit eating.

"I'd be married to him right now but he made me get a divorce. Told me to marry a doctor. That's love."

I nodded again.

"Dumb me," she said wetting her fingers on the Coke bottle, "married a pharmaceutical salesman instead. Trouble is he was selling to more than just doctors and drugstores." She wiped her fingers on her pants. "Took me two babies and a visit from the law to find out. Lost my job at the hospital. Ended up here, flirting with patients and paying two-thirds my paycheck for day care." She smiled, not bitter, just tired. "Ain't that America!"

I miss Robbie Jo. She would have listened, told me what she thought, and made me feel better. She was used to making sick folks feel better. She was trained at tech school, but she had this extra power like Daddy's cousin Zooney. She could talk out the pain. Robbie Jo promised to send her address but she didn't, not before I left. I would have driven 500 miles to see her if I'd only known where.

I needed to talk to someone so much. Donna was out, bless her heart. First of all, she wouldn't understand, and second, she'd tell Andrew. I tried to talk with Aunt Kate a few times, but she just kind of drifted off, reliving her own restlessness I guess. Jack was out from the start. He can't understand anything that isn't in numbers or black-and-white clear. It's as though he doesn't recognize gray and therefore it doesn't exist.

I even thought about Mama. But I knew what she'd say. "Sarah, you need to stay busy-out-of trouble. There's plenty of things you can do." Then she'd suggest a whole stack of projects. And I did try. Home improvement projects, jazz-er-cise, all kinds of volunteer work.

My favorite was cuddling the preemies down at St. Francis. When I went in, the nurse would bathe my arms in disinfectant, dress me in a gown and mask, and send me into the preemie ward sterile as glass. It was a temporary shedding. I felt pure, baptized in alcohol. I'd walk around, choose a baby, and lift it. Each one was like a little bird — warm and jerky, its tiny heart racing. I would cradle it between my breasts against my heart until it relaxed. Then I'd rock and rock until we had reached a spot in the sky with blues and pinks and whispy clouds drifting the same speed of our motion. I loved cuddling those tiny babies. But when I left, all the restlessness would come flooding in, twice as strong, rising around my ankles, above my knees, pulling me away like an ebb tide.

Sometimes it made me think of Judy. The paintings she kept underneath the bed. We met at Mimosa Trailer Park and we used to hang around together on her days off when the guys were somewhere else. On Wednesday nights when Jack was working late and Roy was out trying to sell something, Judy and I'd keep each other company with a few long-neck Buds and a bag of Cheetos. We'd spread two beach towels in front of the couch and watch her tiny TV or just listen to music from the wide gray radio on top of the refrigerator. Judy would dig out a pack of Salems she kept hidden somewhere in the bedroom. Then she'd pull out an ashtray and we'd light up. Pretty soon the filters would turn orange from the Cheetos and the smoke would smell like menthol cheese.

One night when Judy went for a second pack of Salems, she came back dragging a bundled-up blanket.

"Look at these," she said, swaying a little. "This is what I do sometimes." She unwrapped the blanket and released a stack of sunsets, the prettiest ones on canvas you'd ever want to see.

She spread them out on the beach towels and the seat of the couch. In some of the paintings even layers of pastel yellow, lavenders, pinks illuminated the horizon. In others, wild streaks of incendiary oranges, reds, purples shot across the sky so hot it seemed the canvas had burst into flames.

"What makes them so different?" I asked.

Judy chose two, and propped them against her knees. "Dust," she said. "Dust and clouds."

"This one's a sunrise." She pointed to a pastel one and lifted it slightly with her foot. "Gentle, full of hope, like the morning."

"And this one," she said, streaking her hand across the canvas, "is a sunset, full of the day's dust and clouds from the day's heat." She laid the sunrise face down and held the sunset closer to her face. "Dust and clouds shoot light out in a thousand directions." She held up her beer and sucked the bottom out of it, swallowed hard and said, "A really dirty day makes one hell of a sunset." Then she burped loud enough to knock the fake wood off the walls and we burst into giggles. A fit of giggles just like Donna and I used to give each other.

"Why don't you hang them?" I asked.

Judy quit laughing. "Roy won't let me," she said. She stacked the paintings back on the blanket.

I opened and handed her another beer. "Why not?"

Judy slowly pulled each side of the blanket over the canvas until only one lavender corner still showed. "Because," she said, wiping the sweat from the new bottle, "he says painting makes me crazy. I'm really happy while I'm working on it. I get so excited I can't eat or sleep, just plain high, I guess, like a drug. Only better than marijuana or black beauties or anything else I've tried. But when I finish, I start to get sad, then sadder until I get so blue I can't do anything but go to work and come home and cry and go back to work."

Last time I heard from Judy she'd quit painting altogether. "What good is something you love if it makes you crazy?" she wrote. She was still with Roy. I haven't written since I left, but I should. She'd love the sunsets out here. Huge puffy clouds gather over the horizon almost every evening. Some people around here call them storm clouds but they're white, puffier and bigger than any I've seen back home. They roll in at dusk, still white. Then like giant sponges they soak up all the colors of the sunset — reds, oranges, purples — straight up to heaven. I wish Judy could see them and paint one for me.

It's the same feeling I got from those preemies. Happy at first, then too sad for words. I had to quit going. It was in the spring and I kept thinking I'd feel better staying outside. Andrew says, "Light-deprivation induces psychoses," or something like that. He thinks teaching psychology makes him Sigmund Freud Jr. His little snippets of pyscho advice drive me crazy and the rest of the family too. But the benefit of light sounded reasonable so I started hanging around Aunt Kate's farm, roaming around the pasture, trying to soak up warm, bright sanity.

That's when I remembered horses. As kids, Donna and I spent summer after summer at Aunt Kate's farm on top of her two quarter horses, Penelope and Ulysses — Aunt Kate named them herself. Donna always used a saddle. It was black with little silver studs around the back and sides and across the stirrups. The whole saddle really stood out against Penelope's creamy coat. Donna looked like a princess on top of that mare.

But saddles were too boxed in for me. I wanted to feel the horse beneath me, its back smooth and warm against my skin. I rode Ulysses. He was black and he was the fastest. He could stop on a dime. He'd stop so fast I'd flatten out against him and still slide halfway up the crest of his neck. I'd leave Aunt Kate's barn with a layer of dust and sweat and horse hair tatooed inside my thighs. And stay that way until Mama made me wash.

Andrew would probably call that "pubescent sexual displacement." He may be partly right about the displacement. All through high school, whenever I got worried or disappointed or had to cry, I'd go over to Aunt Kate's. I don't like anyone to see me cry. If I cried like Donna, I wouldn't mind. She cries pretty. Little droplets collect in her lashes and sparkle, her cheeks deepen a shade of peach, and her mouth draws up into a little pink blossom. She would have made a perfect soap star, the kind who tears up at the drop of a mate and doesn't even smear her mascara. I cry ugly. My eyes look like they've sunken in and my face turns the color of my hair. So if I felt like crying, I'd run over to Aunt Kate's barn. And after a good sob, I'd hang around the barn, storing up the cool, damp smells of hay and oats and horses, until I felt better.

I quit going to Aunt Kate's barn the summer after high school. Just quit. It was right after the rodeo left town. When I felt like crying, then I'd crawl in the back of the closet, put a towel against my face, and try to sob as softly as I could. Or if Donna was around, I'd take a shower and cry under the faucet. Going to Aunt Kate's barn and being around horses made me sad. Sad like when a really good book ends. You care about the characters and you go through adventures with them and you know what they'd think and do if only they had another murder to solve or sister to avenge or country to reach.

The book ends. You carry them around inside your head for a while. But they're not really yours and they go back to the frontier or the city or the jungle and settle into life without you. Mama always told Donna and me, "Leave while you're having a good time." It never made sense to me, but I guess that's what a really good book does. I tried to do that with Aunt Kate's barn.

I put horses out of my mind when I went to college. That's where I met Jack. He was sure about everything. Not cocky sure, like Andrew, but confident sure. He knew the odds on every football game, who to tip and how much, the best place to buy gas on any given week. I guess it was his confidence that first impressed me. That and how he looked.

He had the clearest bluest eyes, almost translucent, and dark wavy hair. He doesn't have as much hair now, but he hasn't gone bald. Not unless he did after I left. When he let it grow out, it would flip around his ears and kick out on the back of his neck. I loved it that way, but he said it was a nuisance. Jack was tall, almost lanky. He could have played basketball at the college but he was already on an academic scholarship and he didn't want to quit his job at Pettigrew's Appliances. Another thing about Jack. Even back in college he looked comfortable in a suit, not really tailored, just easy.

You couldn't help liking Jack. I think just about everybody in town had something he'd sold them. Toaster, clothes dryer, mixer. When he went to work for Whittaker's Auto-Rama, a lot of his appliance customers followed him. In two years he was making as many sales as some of the men who'd been there a lot longer. Aunt Kate used to say, "That Jack's a natural-born salesman."

When Jack and I started dating he wasn't pushy like the other college guys I went out with, the kind that reach for your breasts before they even kiss you. He was patient. He just kept holding me a little more each date until I was crazy for him. The first time we made love was at his dad's house. His dad had gone bowling. Jack told me he loved me. I didn't say anything back, I just kept pulling him to me and pulling him to me until we couldn't get any closer. Afterwards Jack whispered, "I made a strike!" Sounds silly now, but it was funny at the time and we made a lot of bowling jokes afterwards. Every Tuesday night after that, while Jack's dad was with his league, we were bowling on our own.

Mama and Daddy loved Jack. What parent wouldn't? He was a walking *Consumer Guide*. When Mama needed a new washer he told her which model, what features, and which store had the lowest price. That was over twenty years ago and the thing still washes. It did when I left. And when Daddy wanted a new truck, Jack pulled out a book with dealers' prices, markup, and other information on little lines of coded numbers. Then he drove Daddy around town and helped him pick out a truck. Mama and Daddy seemed relieved when we got married.

Right before our wedding, Daddy said, "Sarah, you hang on to Jack, you hear." Bet he never said that to Donna. Mama just said, "He'll be good for you." She didn't say how. Mama could be cryptic sometimes. But she was right, for a while anyway. For a long while until this restlessness started creeping up on me.

Finally, I started thinking about horses again. Aunt Kate offered her barn, although Penelope and Ulysses were long gone. So I sat down with a red pen and a Farm Market Bulletin and started circling. I found a pretty little roan named Athene. Jack dickered on the price. I think the horse trader got the best of him, mainly because Jack couldn't find a horse consumer guide. He grumbled and grumbled but he bought her. He didn't "mind throwing money away," he said, if it would help me "kick the blues."

And it did for a while until Athene started limping in her left front foot. That's when I met Michael. Bilo's vet didn't treat livestock so he recommended Michael. It's not like I spotted him at a bar or health club or grocery store and brought him home. It just happened. The first time he walked into Aunt Kate's barn, I could almost see electricity in the air, feel it popping all over me. I thought he felt it too, but he acted very professional. He leaned against Athene, his knees slightly bent and pressed together, trapping her hoof between his thighs. "An abscess," he said, not looking up, "she's got an abscess in the outer curve here." I leaned in close, really close, to look but the whole time I was thinking, these are thighs I could kiss. Michael was there a long time. He showed me how to soak her foot in Epsom salts, paint it with iodine, and bandage it with gauze and duct tape. When he got ready to leave he said maybe he'd stop by later in the week to see if I needed any help. He was back the next day. And every day. For a month. In a barn all woodsy and cool.

When I realized what was happening, I tried switching Jack and Michael in my mind, Jack in denim and boots, Michael at the breakfast table eating a grapefruit half with one of those little pointy spoons, like Jack has done every morning of his life as long as I've known him. We must have shared a ton of grapefruit by now. Jack could tell you how many. He'd figure it in his head. Then he'd estimate what the average grapefruit costs and its inflation quota. Jack loves numbers.

Switching men in my mind didn't work. For one thing, Jack's not in the same shape as Michael although he plays basketball once or twice a month with the Chamber of Commerce guys. And Michael would look silly in Jack's loafers.

By then Michael and I had progressed from the stall, to the feed room, to the hay loft. In his arms I was warm and comfortable and more alive than I'd been in years.

But Michael decided to leave. He said he didn't want to have to sneak around to be with me, and he couldn't handle the thought of me in Jack's bed. But I think his leaving was just as much restlessness. The morning he came to tell me goodbye, the pasture was saturated with rain and the lot looked like the pond. We'd had a downpour most of two days. But as the clouds lifted, the mountain ridge behind the farm shone the bluest I'd ever seen it, cobalt blue. So blue I wanted to run straight into those mountains before the color paled a single shade. Still I didn't plan on going with Michael until the last minute. Like when a plane slips out of a cloud and crosses you and you wonder what if you were up there in it looking down. I had to know "what if."

I didn't leave a note. How do you say, "I love you but I'm leaving with another man. XXX"? And to be honest, I didn't want to think too much. I learned early how to blank out pain with my mind. I'd pretend to be out of my body, just watching. Like those people you read about who are clinically dead but come back to life. It usually works for me. Except with the babies.

It's been a year worth remembering, of being in the book instead of reading it. I've tried to store up everything — like the hills in

Tennessee and the sand storms in Texas and the dry winds in Arizona. On our way through Oklahoma we saw a sundog, a tiny rainbow almost in a circle just above the horizon. Michael said it was a reflection of the sun and it usually meant bad weather. But I imagined a huge rainbow behind a little round tear in the sky, so you only got a glimpse of the colors from this side.

I'm pregnant again. Don't know which I'll lose first, the baby or Michael. He's like me — born restless. We had to leave Athene in Tennessee. Michael says he'll go get her soon but I'm thinking I should sell her. Don't know what she'll bring now. Jack could tell me to the dollar. Maybe I'll give her away then go back home.

If I do go home, I'll have to tell Jack something, most likely in numbers. Maybe that my hormones were up 65 percent and made me crazy. Andrew will agree with that, I'm sure, and probably provide a lecture on the female hormone condition and its psychological consequences. I won't tell Mama or Daddy anything. Because Daddy won't be able to understand and I think Mama's been mind-traveling for years on her own. Donna will just be glad to see me.

But I wish I could tell them the truth. If I knew the truth. I've been thinking about it the whole year and I still can't give an exact reason for leaving. I can tell them it's like you're in halves and neither side fits. Or that for once in my life I had to do something crazy to feel alive. Or that I need this one year — right or wrong — to think about for the next forty. If I can make them understand, maybe I will too. Then I can go home.

PART II

FUNERAL

DONNA

Mama would be proud, really proud to see all these people teary eyed for her. The flowers! Daddy told Maurice down at the florist to let people send nothing but gardenias. They're all over the place — the choir loft, the communion railing, the window sills — every space where somebody's not sitting or standing. And the food! We had fourteen cakes, seven casseroles, eight gallons of tea, and a whole pan of ham biscuits as of this morning. Mrs. Lois Turpin's at the house, keeping a list. Andrew says we handle grief by eating ourselves silly. I asked him what did they do up in Massachusetts? Drink themselves silly?

It's good to have Sarah home. I'm not even mad at her anymore. I mean how could I be with her looking so bad? Nobody's blaming her. At least, nobody's said so. Still, I wonder if she'd come home a little earlier, but that's water over the well.

Sarah's last letter had a return address in tiny boxy letters across the back of the envelope. Andrew said it was a sign that she wanted to be found. He can analyze handwriting. He said he could see it in the way she signed her name too. But I still don't think she would have come home except for Mama.

Mama wasn't the same after Sarah left, though she didn't say much about Sarah. It was more like she was shrinking. She was already little, smaller in the waist than me. Of course, she didn't have two babies at the same time. But Sarah's the same way. She took after Mama. I took after Daddy's side. Granny Crawford was big as the side of the barn before she died. That's scary! I'm thinking about signing up for aerobics down at the Y. Andrew says I should, not because I need it but because I'd feel better. But I was too worried about Mama at the time. She didn't go out as much, or talk as much, or do anything as much. I tried to talk to

Daddy but he wasn't any help. He just stayed busy fertilizing or staking his tomatoes or mulching. Andrew said they both needed to get away. The only thing I could think of was Florida.

They used to talk about going to Florida. Especially when somebody from the church came home showing Disney World postcards or photographs from Sea World or handing out oranges. Andrew and I finally talked Daddy into taking Mama to Orlando. Daddy said he didn't care one thing about Disney World but he'd like to see how they grew oranges in those groves and he wouldn't mind walking through Sea World while he was there.

Mama didn't seem to care one way or the other, but I went down to Swirl's and bought her some new cotton shifts, a pair of light weight pants, a T-shirt with waves on it, and some tennis shoes. They were navy blue with rope like trim around the edges and they fit just fine. I packed my suitcase for her and tried to tell her how pretty and different everything was in Florida. I'd been once. With Andrew on our honeymoon. I still have my mouse ears.

Mama and Daddy were gone less than a week but when they got back both of them were like kids, talking about what they'd seen and done. Mama's hands were flying. "We thought we'd never get there," she said. "Joe drove and drove and drove before we even got to Florida and then we were only halfway to Orlando."

"Thought we'd never get there," Daddy echoed. "You wouldn't believe the orange groves on this side of R-land-o, all gone to root."

"Orlando," Andrew said.

"Yea," Daddy said, "all gone to root. A real shame. I asked some feller taking money on the pike."

"Turnpike?" Andrew said.

"Yea, I asked the feller on the pike why the groves were like that." Daddy rubbed his palms together. "Know what he said?"

" 'Move along, sir'?" Andrew said, cutting his eyes at me. He was starting to fidget.

"Yea, but before that, he said they got froze out five years ago. Said the growers just let those orange trees go."

"Sea World was really something," Mama said.

"Ex-pen-sive!" Daddy said, stretching his arms like a preacher.

"But I had those $2.50-off coupons," Mama said to Daddy. "Lonita gave them to us," she told Andrew and me.

"It was still $50 to get in," Daddy said, looking straight at Mama. "But I guess it was worth it." Mama smiled.

"I took all kinds of pictures in Sea World," she said. "Joe did too but his camera got ruined."

"It wasn't much of a camera, anyway," Daddy said, "the one I got at the Jocky Lot. I give five dollars."

"What happened to it?" Andrew asked. Daddy didn't answer.

"There was this sign," Mama said, " 'Splash Area.' You know how Joe is." She patted his shoulder. "He thinks signs don't apply if you don't read them out loud." Daddy grinned a little. "The first time Shamu turned a flip," Mama said, "Joe got soaked. I was up higher in the stands. I snapped him just as the water knocked his hat off. Hope the picture turns out." She was laughing now.

"Ruint my camera," Daddy said. "But it wasn't worth much. 'Cept the film. It was Kodak." He rested his hands on his belly.

"What got me was the way those Shamus swam and jumped together, Donna, side by side, like they were joined," Mama said.

"They were huge, Donna Jean," Daddy interrupted. "Bigger than Jaws! You wouldn't believe how much water they knocked out."

"We saw them too, on our honeymoon," Andrew said.

"Yea, but that was years ago." Daddy shoved his hands in his pockets. "They've grown since then."

"Watching them flip and twist and jump together," Mama said, "made me wonder why people can't be more like that." She hesitated. "Take Sarah and Jack for instance." Daddy didn't look up. "I couldn't help thinking," Mama went on, "that if they'd go down there to Orlando, like on a second honeymoon, they could work out their problems."

"I don't know," Andrew said. "Vacations don't always bring out the best in a family. I mean there's only one bathroom, and somebody gets sick, nobody agrees on where to eat, and the water tastes funny."

I knew he was talking about taking me and the twins to Cherry Grove Beach last summer. "And," I said, looking straight at Andrew, "somebody kicks the mattress."

"You're right about the water," Daddy said. "That Florida water tastes like a frog in the well. Vivienne filled up a thermos jug in case the car ran hot. It holds two gallons slap full and we drank the whole thing before we got out of R-land-o. Don't know what we'd of done if the engine run hot. At Sea World a little cup of Pepsi-Cola costs a dollar, and you won't believe what one chocolate chip cookie costs."

"But they were the biggest cookies I've ever seen," Mama said, spreading her fingers, "Big as a saucer."

"Bigger than the head on Kate's barn cat," Daddy said. "I'm thinking of taking Vivienne to Dollywood next year. Now that we know how to act."

It was so good to see Mama and Daddy looking happy again. Mama even got back to what she called her busy work. For a while.

Seems like a lifetime ago. With Mama stretched out in that box and Daddy crying like a baby. He wanted to have her buried in her Orlando outfit — those pants and the T-shirt with waves on it. I told him everybody would think we were loony. But I gave in on the tennis shoes. They didn't show. Neither did the dolphin. It satisfied Daddy though. I swear I feel more like his mama than his daughter. Like Granny Crawford. My Lord, what a thought! But I've got Mama's genes too. Busy genes.

When Sarah and I were growing up, Mama kept some kind of project going all the time. In the summer, she'd be freezing corn and lima beans and soup mix, until you couldn't get in the kitchen for steam and hot smells and little plastic bags all over the place. In the winter she'd sew — dresses, blouses, coats prettier than you could buy in a store. And they were done up so neatly, Aunt Kate said we could have worn them inside out. In the spring and fall, she'd find old pieces of furniture to refinish. I tried to help once, but the chemical stuff she stripped off the old finish with was so strong you'd have to wear rubber gloves and scrub with steel wool until it felt like your arms were coming off, and the whole time you'd be smelling that stripper stuff till you got high as a TV antenna. But Mama kept at it until she was convinced she'd brought it "back to life," she'd say. And she would. There was an old washstand that must have been in somebody's coal cellar for years. But she had it looking so good I was happy to put it in my own dining room. I set geraniums on it in the summer. And she did a sideboard for Sarah and Jack that would bring no telling what. Jack said $1000. He looked it up in some antique book and told Mama.

The summer before I got married, Mama and Daddy painted the entire house inside out. Mama made new curtains for the front hall and sitting room, and recovered the living room sofa in peachy fabric with little flowers woven in. Andrew couldn't believe how hard she worked.

Mama was busy, even sitting. If she was carrying on a conversation, she'd be polishing silver or folding towels or peeling apples. During Sunday dinner she'd be up and down, seeing if anybody needed anything. If Sarah or I had Sunday dinner, Mama would stay at the table. But the whole time she'd be folding her napkin until it was so small you could have fit it in a matchbox. That was Mama. High strung, Daddy called it.

And for a while after the Florida trip, she was back to normal. But about the time Andrew told me he'd turn orange if he heard "R-land-o" again, Mama quit talking about it. I guess the fun wore off like a finished project. She started shrinking again. Not just her body, but her whole world. She slept later, read more, didn't go to Sunday school, didn't cook as much, quit sewing altogether. And she watched more TV than she ever had before — mostly reruns of old westerns. I tried to look after her and Daddy too. I started talking about Dolly Parton this and Dolly Parton that, thinking I could get them interested in Dollywood. I told Daddy about the folks running her big ole bra up the flag pole when she was there. And I told Mama about all the craftsmen she could watch and talk to and get ideas for new projects. But it didn't work. Daddy kept gardening and Mama kept shrinking.

One day, Daddy said it was right after "Gunsmoke," Mama keeled over. He said it was the episode where Miss Kitty is kidnapped and Matt Dillion thinks he's lost her for sure. Daddy said Mama just bowed forward, rolled onto the floor, gentle-like, and curled up. He got her to the hospital and the doctor said she'd had a stroke.

Mama never did come conscious again, not really, except for calling out some names we'd never heard of. Mrs. Lois Turpin, who was sitting with her one afternoon, thought Mama was speaking in tongues. But I don't totally trust Mrs. Lois in religious matters, considering she drives around town with a license tag that says "I M SAVD." Aunt Kate said she knew Mama wasn't talking in tongues, but didn't tell us who the names were. Daddy didn't say anything but seemed awfully upset.

I wrote Sarah right away and told her about Mama. She called me on the phone and asked me to pick her up at the airport. Now, I was missing her terribly and couldn't wait to see her but I hate driving that interstate. Since they raised the speed limit back up to 65-mph, every truck in the universe uses that highway. And I had the girls and Mama to help with and Daddy too. So I sent Andrew.

I knew Sarah would be glad to see him, and she knows airports make me nervous. I've only flown once and that was years ago when I went to meet Andrew's folks.

Actually I kind of enjoyed the flying part but what I couldn't stand was taking off. My stomach churned and my ears buzzed and I felt all panicky. But the rest was fine. Except the airport in Boston. It was so crowded that you could get lost without taking a step. But it was old hat to Andrew. That's what I love about him. Nothing seems to shake him. Unless you count seeing me in labor.

The girls look real sweet today but they don't know what's going on. You never do as a child. I wanted to get them black dresses but you can't hardly find plain black for children. Anyway, Andrew wouldn't hear to it. Had a fit, I mean. I had to settle on navy blue shifts with big white collars and red bows. Cut the bows off. Andrew didn't want me to cut off the bows. I told him I could sew them back on for later. I haven't seen him this fidgety since I went into labor.

I didn't want him to see me flat on my back with my feet in those stirrups, but he wanted to do natural childbirth "for bonding," he said, so we went through all these classes. But I've got to tell you, when the first pain hit, it was goodbye La Maze! Hello Demerol! The only time in my life I begged for a needle. The nurse told me afterward that not only did Andrew puke on his shoes but he nearly fainted when he saw there were twins. That was before they started doing ultrasound on everybody and her cousin, so twins were a real surprise to us. Scarlet and Charlotte. I named one and Andrew named the other.

I had my tubes tied right then and there, and Andrew didn't complain. He was real good about not bothering me for a while. Guess he was scared my tubes might come undone. I kind of hated not having a boy for Daddy but Sarah was still trying then. Don't know if any of hers were boys or not. She lost them so early. Except for one and they never did say which it was.

I didn't tell anybody but Andrew that Sarah was coming home. I was afraid she'd change her mind at the last minute. Sarah does that sometimes.

One time was when she and Nancy Lou decided to pierce their ears. Nancy Lou was her best friend in high school. Sarah knew not to ask Mama because she would say, "Only cheap girls had pierced ears when I was growing up." First Nancy Lou and Sarah were going to this woman who pierces ears and reads palms, then they decided to use needles and bottle corks, then somebody told them you could get this device that pressed a hole through your earlobe while you slept. They went on for days and days trying to decide which method to use and whether they were going through with it or not. They gave up on the sleeping device because no one except somebody's cousin in New York had actually used it. Then one day Nancy Lou came in with earrings on and said she did it by herself. She used an ice cube to get her lobes all numb then she pushed her mother's embroidery needle through real fast before the feeling came back. That's all it took for Sarah.

She got a pack of needles, a tray of ice, and started numbing. Nancy Lou told her the needle had to be boiling hot to react properly with the cold lobe. But by the time Sarah had a pan of water bubbling, the feeling was back in her ears so she started again. Then the needle would cool off and she'd have to reheat the water. She was down to her last ice cube when she got the two together. Nancy Lou put ink dots on Sarah's ears, like tiny blue moles, and Sarah gave the needle a shove. I swear to you, I heard it crunch. They say I didn't because I had my face in a pillow but I did and I gagged.

Sarah didn't cry but she said it hurt bad and she just started holding onto Nancy Lou and shaking, trying to get the pain out of her mind. She shook so hard she knocked Nancy Lou's earrings clean off. I say "off" not "out" because that's when we discovered Nancy Lou had glued a bead to the front of each earlobe. I think if Sarah's ear wasn't hurting so bad she'd have pierced Nancy Lou's for real.

Sarah kept her earlobe hidden except for dousing it in alcohol every night until it grew back. I couldn't believe it but she still wanted pierced ears. She finally asked Mama. And Mama surprised us both by saying "yes," if Dr. Sams did it. Sarah came home swinging these big loops and saying it hardly hurt at all this time. I didn't want mine pierced though. I was afraid of scar tissue. There was a girl in school whose smallpox shot ate up her arm. The last time I saw her, the scar was moving up her neck. I didn't want an earlobe to do that or come out looking like a squash. No thank you.

So I didn't tell anybody else that Sarah was coming home. I figured that was a lot more painful than sticking a needle through her lobe. And she might change her mind. But I suppose I should have told Jack.

He just walked in. Wouldn't have seen him except for his height. Saw the top half of his head. Hair needs a good cut. It's waved out here and poking out there like he washed it and went to bed with it wet. He worked his way in right smack behind Sarah. I don't think she knows he's there. I'd tell her if she'd look this way. I'd point or cut my eyes or something but she's staring straight off into space.

I haven't seen Jack since I showed him Sarah's first few letters. He said they were forged. They weren't, because Andrew had already checked them out. I ran into Joanne again at the Dixie store and she said Jack was doing better. I didn't ask how she knew. And you can't believe everything she says, anyway. She believes that stuff she reads in her checkout line. Some of it may be true, like flying saucers. I mean, who knows? But she believes freaky stuff like Elvis's face sighted on moon. Still I guess I could have called Jack or invited him back to Sunday dinner. I asked Andrew and he said we should just play it by ear, like I do the piano.

Anyway, I sent Andrew to get Sarah at the airport. That was the day before Mama died. While he was gone I baked a double recipe of fudge-turtle brownies. What you do is make brownie batter and then use a whole bag of vanilla caramels in a middle layer. And when it bakes and you cut it in squares, the warm caramel runs out like tiny legs so that each piece looks like a little brown turtle. Like I tell Andrew, you have to use your imagination. He never can see the turtle. He sees other things like mud puddles and lumps of coal but never a turtle. Even when I point out the head and legs and tiny little tail, he still can't see it. He's alway worrying about cholesterol too and says I shouldn't make desserts. But I had to do something waiting on Sarah and worrying about Mama. It was Mama's recipe. She used to make a pan of fudge-turtle brownies every time we were going on vacation. Sarah and I would sit in the back seat and sneak them out of an old cookie tin that said ''Imported for your good taste,'' until our fingers were stickier than our mouths.

Andrew said Sarah didn't say much on the trip home from the airport except how was Mama and me and the twins, and she talked about new buildings along the interstate. He brought her here to our house. She wanted to go straight to the hospital but he thought she should see me first. He was right, of course.

I have to tell you I didn't know how I was going to act. I mean since Sarah left and Mama started shrinking, I had to do everything for her and Daddy. Get the groceries, do the laundry, cook Sunday dinner. Like I didn't have a life of my own. And here was Sarah off having the time of her life with some mystery man. I haven't had a soul to talk to except Andrew and he's not the best listener. For the first time in my life I was mad at Sarah, really mad. I planned not to hug her or anything. Just sit her down, offer her some tea, and tell her what I thought. I must have eaten four fudge turtles planning my speech. But when I saw Sarah all I could do was hug her and cry and hug her some more. I missed her so much.

Wish Daddy would be quiet. There's something about a man crying too sad for words. I pressed his suit, but I swear, it looks like he's been rolling around in it. Dear Lord, I'm tired. Too tired to cry. I feel as tired as Mama looked right before. I can't believe she's gone. Wonder if strokes are hereditary. I'd better get some rest. I'm going to get that makeover I've been promising myself, I don't care what it costs. That and about a week of doing as little as possible. Andrew will have to look after the girls. Tenure or no tenure, he'll have to spend some time at home for a change. Look at Sarah. Pale as a ghost. It must run in the family.

ANDREW

A dozen-cake funeral, maybe more. Donna can tell you exactly. And will. That and who brought what dish and what's special about each recipe and where she last tasted it. Food is as important as lineage around here.

Yesterday Donna was running around making sure everybody who came by got a wedge of cake or hot biscuit or cold tea. And last night after the funeral home, she insisted on pulling it all back out "just in case" she said. She was right. Enough people came by to polish off another cake. You can bet, as soon as this is over today the food will come back out for hungry mourners.

Not that I'm making light of the occasion. But I'm not sure food didn't have something to do with Vivienne's condition. All that canning and freezing and cooking and jumping up during meals to bring in more eventually wore her out. Not that Sarah's escapade didn't contribute to it.

Sarah's feeling it too. She's hanging on to the back of that pew like the floor might fall away.

When Donna asked me to meet Sarah at the airport, she made some excuse for not going herself. But I know why she wanted me to go. I'm a good listener. She knew I'd be able to talk with Sarah on a nonthreatening level, without the bonds of kinship to raise the emotional pitch. I was the best choice. Donna's smart that way. She acts a little addled at times but that's a persona, you understand, a role her family has always expected of her and therefore she performs for them. Unconscious, maybe, but a role nevertheless. Hell, all of them have these roles.

Take Sunday dinner. It's a ritual. At least it was before Sarah's departure and Vivienne's stroke. This is the way it went. Joe would start it by asking the blessing — "Bless this food to the nourishment of our bodies. Amen." Sometimes he asked Jack to bless it and Jack said the same thing. I would have varied it a little, made it reflect the weather or the situation of one of the family members or something about world peace, for God's sake! But that would break the ritual. Donna always asked, "Mama, does it matter where we sit?" and Vivienne always answered "no," and then we all sat where we always sat — Joe at the head, Vivienne at the end closest to the kitchen, Donna and I on one side, Jack and Sarah on the other. When Kate was there she wedged a chair in anywhere she wanted to and nobody complained. She's the only one who could break the ritual but that's her role too. The ritual-breaker.

Joe would start the meat while the rest of us grabbed whatever bowl or platter was in front of us. After everything went around, Joe would storm his food with a layer of salt so thick it left a grainy white halo on the table around his plate. I've tried to warn him about high sodium intake, but he pretends he doesn't hear me. That's part of his persona — he's hard of hearing when he doesn't want to listen.

Then conversations would start, the women usually talking about this aunt or that cousin or when Donna and Sarah were growing up. Joe always dominated the men's conversation with some gardening advice or questions for Jack about the price on something he wanted to buy — like a yard tractor or a lawn mower. All conversations would go on simultaneously. It was maddening. Joe would be saying something and Donna would turn to me with the tail end of some gossip she'd just heard. Then Vivienne would ask me right in the middle of both if I needed more ice. I wanted to jump up, I don't know how many times, and scream, "Hell no! I don't need anything but some sanity around here!"

Of course, I wouldn't do that to Vivienne. She was a nice lady, pretty for her age, but so busy. I never saw her sit through an entire meal.

The idea of her lying still in that casket is mind-boggling. I don't believe I've ever seen her still for more than five seconds at a time.

When we were first married, I told Donna her mother's busyness was an escape mechanism. Donna said, "Escape from what? Mama's always been busy." I guess it's hard to see personality disorders in your own parents, but I could sure see it in Vivienne. Up and down, pouring tea, getting more hot rolls, bringing in dessert.

Dessert. That's another food fettish. If you don't want dessert, you'd better say you're highly allergic to it and your throat will close up if you eat a single bite. If you say, "No thank you," they'll say, "Oh, have some." If you hesitate for a second, they take that as "Yes, I'd love a huge serving." If you say, "No" another time, they think you mean "Just a medium piece, please." And if you don't eat all of it, you'll get, "What's wrong? Don't you like it?" After months of this, Joe finally told me, "I know your problem. You're allergic to natural foods like sugar and honey and cream. What'd they feed you up there, anyhow?" I realize by now I have a role too, that bastard of a son-in-law from Massachusetts.

Donna's role at Sunday dinner was to keep some banter going and to say things like "Mama, the rice isn't sticky, it's just fine," or "Daddy, these tomatoes are so sweet and juicy! Did you grow them?" Sarah's role at first was to laugh occasionally and turn her eyes to Jack. But the last few years that changed. She didn't have much to say, as if she were ill at ease half the time. At one point I almost felt a kinship, but her uneasiness was different. Just before she left, she would sit through the entire dinner without a word. I couldn't believe that no one else noticed it. Too busy in their own roles, maybe.

Then there's Jack. You'd have thought he was blood kin the way Joe used to treat him. He's smart, I'll admit. But it's all in sales. I never could put him and Sarah together. She's better suited to a musician or mime or circus performer or obviously a large-animal veterinarian, than to a rotarian president.

Donna says Jack will be here, but I haven't seen him. She doesn't miss a face. This place is packed, but she'll go through who's here and what they're wearing and where they're sitting. I wonder if Jack will sit with the family, if he comes.

I've not seen him in a year or more. He and Sarah used to come over every week. Jack beat me on "The Price Is Right" a time or two, but I took him on "Jeopardy" every time unless they had a car category like Autos of the '50s. That's what we used to do when Sarah and Jack came over. Donna and Sarah would go to the kitchen and talk or take care of the twins, while Jack and I played gameshows. They quit coming over. Donna said she thought Jack was too busy at the car lot. I thought he might just be tired of my beating him at Jeopardy. But I guess he was busy. And to be honest, he's done well. From salesman to head man. But the thing that gets me is, while he was talking his way up the dealership ladder and getting more money at every rung, I was paying out money and working my ass off to get a Ph.D. Seven years, it took me, mainly because I taught a full load the whole time. Three classes every semester, and one each session of summer school, too.

The whole time Donna was after me to let her have a baby. "Just one," she'd say, "just one." Then she'd hang all over me and kiss my neck and rub against me. We couldn't afford a hamster much less a baby. But I promised her the day I got my hands on that sheepskin that said "Andrew Webster, Ph.D." she could throw her pills out the window. She did. And I had her pumped up within a month. Even I couldn't believe I'd get her pregnant so fast. Joe and Vivienne seemed happy and upset at the same time, maybe because of Sarah's miscarriages. I tried to tell Jack and Sarah to go to a specialist, but Sarah seemed to think if she tried harder she could have one, and Jack, I think, had lost interest by then.

Donna's "just one" came out two. I helped deliver them. I never saw so much blood and mess. Being a doctor of psychology doesn't really prepare you. It was a long time before I wanted to make love again. Of course, Donna was in no condition for a while. But even after she was, I kept dreaming those coiled up umbilical cords were wrapped around my throat. Not exactly an erotic dream. I finally got over it. Now I have that dream only once or twice a year.

I feel it in here though, as if I'm drowning in a sea of females. Kate and Sarah and Donna and the twins all sucking the air right out of my lungs.

I named one of the twins Charlotte after my mother, and Donna named the other one Scarlet because she said "It rhymes." That's they way they talk and hear around here. Donna can't hear the difference between "pen" and "pin." None of them can. They're not too particular about getting the right pronunciation of a word as long as they understand each other. But some words they're really picky about, especially if they consider them to be signs of manners.

I still call Joe, Mr. Crawford to his face. Did the same with Vivienne. And that's after knowing them all these years. Right after Donna and I were married, I called them by their first names. You would have thought I proposed incest. Donna said it just sounded a little strange, my being younger. She tried to get me to call them Mama and Daddy. That didn't work either. Now the twins call them Mama C. and Daddy C. which is all right with the Crawfords. But they have their own standard of propriety and etiquette around here that is unlike the rest of the country, the world for that matter.

That's just the way these people are, and sometimes it takes an unencumbered observer to recognize it. Take the civil war at the fire station. When I was first dating Donna, all Mr. Crawford could talk about was the mess at the volunteer fire station, and his garden, of course. For several months, the community had a problem with fires — brush piles, open fields, vacant tenant houses, that sort of thing.

Then one night, Mr. Crawford caught a boy in the middle of a field with a gasoline can in hand. The boy ran away but not before Mr. Crawford recognized him. The fire chief's son. Then the proverbial ash can hit the fan. When Mr. Crawford reported his findings, the chief denied it, his son denied it, and half the firemen couldn't believe it. The other half not only believed it but wanted the boy publicly whipped.

I tried to explain to Donna's father that whether the fire chief denied it or not, he'd keep an eye on his son and the fires would stop. And as for the boy, the fires were probably a plea for attention. But Mr. Crawford insisted that he had been called a liar and as far as the boy's need for attention went, a public whipping would work just dandy. You can't tell Joe anything. At least I can't. Donna said, "It's not what you say, Andrew, but the way you say it. Daddy doesn't trust anyone with an accent." As if he speaks the King's English.

Donna's not that stubborn. She usually listens to reason. That's more than I can say for the rest of them. Not that the Crawfords aren't smart. At least the women, they all read. And Donna's Aunt Kate is almost a scholar. I enjoy talking philosophy with Kate. She says literature is truer than history, and she has a point, although she oversimplifies. But she's a little loosely woven sometimes, morally speaking. She goes through boyfriends as fast as she reads novels. Not the best example for Sarah and Donna, growing up. She hasn't had one around lately. Thank God. The twins were beginning to wonder why Aunt Kate had so many men and no husband. I told her what they said. She said to tell them she hadn't found one with a long enough plot. She didn't crack a smile, as though it were the normal way to behave and she wondered why I asked.

She's not shedding a tear this morning, but she looks hungover. I suppose she tied one on last night. It's her grief release mechanism — superior, if you ask me, to stuffing one's face. She's not wearing black either, thank God. Donna is. I've never seen her in black up close to her face like that. Something about women in black that sets me on edge. Like boards on an old house, burned tree stumps, coal. I don't like Donna in black. Not even black underwear. She belongs in soft blues and yellows and pinks.

Donna was wearing a pink evening gown the first time I saw her. Every summer the town organizers have some kind of festival. My first year here, it was a peach festival to increase sales for the fruit growers and local merchants. These people can't have a festival without a beauty pageant, whether it's Miss Peanut, Miss Pork, Little Miss Water Fall or whatever they're celebrating. This is where I came in. My being from Massachusetts and a psychology professor and a bachelor at the time evidently made me a likely candidate for judge. I'd never even been to a beauty pageant before, but I'd helped judge a science fair and a few declamation contests, so I supposed there wouldn't be too much to it.

The pageant started at 6:00 which I thought was a little early until I found out we had to select Miss Wee Blossom and Little Miss Nectarine before the main event, Miss Peach Queen, even started. By 8:30 I was sick of crinolines, whining children, and weeping mothers. If I had thought it wouldn't affect my chance for tenure, I'd have walked out. But then they brought out the older girls, ones who'd undergone puberty. I relaxed a little and started enjoying the view. The first eleven contestants ranged from mildly cute to quite pretty. But the twelfth one looked like a P.E. coach with a wig. That's who I thought it was at first, a clown of sorts to ease the tension. I laughed out loud. Alone. No one else was laughing. I couldn't believe it. I asked the judge next to me who number twelve was. He said it was Crystabelle Dean. We weren't supposed to know their names so I asked him how he knew. He said everybody in town knew her, her four brothers, her father, and her uncle in prison. All wrestlers, professional, including Crystabelle.

Now I didn't know if he was kidding or not but I didn't laugh anymore when she came out on stage, not even when she modeled her Jantzen swimsuit and the little diving girl insignia was stretched horizontally instead of vertically, not even when Crystabelle played "Old Black Joe" on a handsaw. Nobody did. We all clapped and looked straight ahead.

The one bright spot that got me through the night was watching Donna on stage. She was beautiful. She had a perfect little coed figure back then. Every outfit was pink, even her swimsuit and she had a little gait in that swimsuit that made me want to jump up and chase her behind the curtain. She played "Exodus" for her talent, mostly one-handed, but with such passion I almost had goose-bumps. I didn't know her then but I knew I would very soon. She won Miss Peach Queen. The decision was unanimous and every judge except me had Crystabelle as first runner-up. I held out for second runner-up as a matter of principle.

That's the way I met Donna. Love at first sight. Strange thing for a doctor of psychology to admit, but it's true. If I could have gotten over her after I met the rest of the family, believe me, I would have. But she was so sweet and soft and sexy in a prissy kind of way that I had to marry her. I took her for better and the rest of the Crawfords for worse.

I hate funerals. Not that anybody likes them, except Lois Turpin and morticians. For me, they're suffocating, a black sea of emotion. Reminds me of my father's funeral. Mama, Nana, Aunt Ruth, all in black and all around me. I couldn't see beyond black. I was no older than the twins. The only child of a dead man. And suddenly expected to become one's own father, reincarnate.

Sarah looks as though she's suffocating too. Hers has another source: guilt, I would venture a guess. As a professional, I sympathize. As brother-in-law, well . . . I'll admit to some resentment.

I knew Sarah was ready to come home, and I told Donna that very fact. Vivienne's illness was the perfect excuse, not that I don't think Sarah loved her mother, as much as she could love anyone other than herself. I told Donna that too, but she didn't like me saying Sarah was selfish. But she knows I'm right. I'm proficient at analyzing handwriting. Sarah's t's are prime examples of self-centeredness. Your t's tell on you.

I'm right about her being ready to come home, too. She probably was bored with the vet and got enough roaming around. Her hormones have no doubt started to settle back down, leaving her less sexually inclined and more domestic. Not that she couldn't control her actions. What she did was totally selfish and without regard as to what it would do to the rest of the Crawfords. Look at Vivienne. She already had problems but not this bad. Joe has become even more disagreeable and hard of hearing. And Jack. I never have thought he deserved his success but he certainly didn't deserve this either. I don't see how he's kept his dealership going all year. I haven't seen him since before Sarah left. He doesn't come around here or to Joe's at all. Everyone thought he and Joe were so close. It's as if Sarah were their sole connection.

Donna and I have suffered the worst. Donna depended on Sarah so much for girl talk. Now she stores up bits and pieces all day long and unloads them on me with no thought to rhyme, reason, or chronological order. She's had to take over her parents' household and I've had to just about take over ours. Or I would have if it weren't for this tenure project hanging over me. I haven't decided what it is yet, but I have to come up with something soon or I'll miss my chance.

As for sex, you can forget that at our house. For example, last Thursday, Donna came in tired and grumpy. She'd been at Joe's house and then taken the twins to register for school; unfortunately, Charlotte was sick, and Scarlet had piano lessons. I'd been at the library researching ideas for my project, and when I came home, quite understandably, Donna didn't have dinner prepared. But I didn't complain. I knew she'd had a hard day as soon as I stepped inside the doorway and she started down the list. Not exactly down the list, more here and there and back again.

Then she said, "Am I getting fat?"

"No," I told her. "You don't need to gain any, but you're fine, especially for a woman your age who's had twins." Then I offered to rub her back, that's all, just rub her back. She wouldn't let me touch her.

"Rub yourself!" she snapped and went to bed.

That's not like my Donna. It's this Sarah thing that's done it to her. Kate's the only one who hasn't suffered, and I swear, I think she was happy for Sarah. Kate's a little unbalanced at times; I can see it in her signature.

So I had mixed emotions when Donna said Sarah was coming back. I knew there'd be problems. Yet I was relieved for Donna to have another confidant and some help with their parents. When I met Sarah at the airport, she seemed glad enough to see me although a little disappointed that Donna didn't come. She looked about the same, a little thinner maybe but still attractive, not as pretty as my Donna but handsome in her own way.

I explained her mother's condition and offered my theory on what caused her illness: lack of calcium, hormonal change, delayed empty-nest syndrome. I didn't mention that her eldest daughter's desertion probably accelerated the whole thing. If Sarah was upset, I couldn't detect it because she kept her head turned, looking out the window most of the trip home.

Something about her at that angle reminded me of her mother, the only time I'd seen much of a resemblance of Sarah to any of the family. They're smaller, more blond and pixie-like, even Joe. Sarah never seemed to fit the Crawford mold before, but for the first time I could see her mother in her. The way the light played off her cheekbone and down her neck, if I were a painter I'd have a word for it. An aura of sorts. She reminded me of a melancholy song without lyrics, one in which you feel the singer's sadness without knowing why. I wondered if Sarah had ever been happy or ever would be.

She has that same expression now, more than a funeral look. Thank God, my Donna's not like that, but I need to get her out of that awful black dress.

SARAH

Dear God, it's hot in here. I'd forgotten how they pack in for funerals. Daddy's so slumped over, nothing in his suit hangs right. It almost looks empty. He's sobbing like he did at Donna's wedding. Only worse. He's not trying to hide it. Aunt Kate is stone-faced. Cried herself out last night. Donna's pretty as ever, even in black. She has a twin at each hand. Andrew looks like he might conduct the service. I can't believe Donna's held up so well, but then she doesn't have the guilt that I do.

When I got her letter, I felt a sensation I'd shut out for an entire year. Raw, unhomogenized guilt. Like morning sickness, starting in the pit of my stomach then rising up my throat through my nostrils, all hot and burny making me feel like a volcano. Guilt does that to me.

Guilt about Mama almost opened a floodgate for what I'd done to the rest of this family the past year. Especially Jack. Sometimes I'd see his face in my mind, his clear blue eyes all red and puffy as though he'd rolled in oats. But I wouldn't let myself deal with more than one guilt at a time and Mama is it. I wanted to thank her for everything she'd done for me and apologize for everything I'd done to her. Like the times I disappointed her or made her cry or said I hated her.

It's so hot. I wish Kate would move over just a little.

When Donna and I were little, it seemed like we were always getting shots for one thing or another. If I felt sick, I'd hide in my room or at Aunt Kate's house. But Mama would figure it out, find me, and take me to Dr. Sams. "Penicillin," he'd say, every time. And out would come the hypodermic. Donna didn't like penicillin shots any better than I did. She simply couldn't hide anything. And even if we weren't sick, there'd be a vaccination or booster shot due. Mama wouldn't tell us until we were almost there. Then she'd take us into the office, one at each hand. Donna would go in sniffling and clinging to Mama's arm. But I'd hang back, dig my heels in, make Mama pull me through the doorway.

Dr. Sams liked to give his own shots. He had a system for children. He'd turn his hypodermic hand in, the needle pointing toward himself, as though you couldn't see it. He'd bounce the back of his hand on your forearm, saying, "Here comes the bunny. Hop . . . Hop . . . Hop!" On the third hop he'd swing the needle around and shove the point dripping into your arm. Then he'd hand you a lollipop. One morning he did just that — the hopping and all. When he handed me the lollipop, a green one, I wouldn't lift my good arm to take it. Mama said, "Take it, Sarah, and tell Dr. Sams 'thank you.'" My punctured arm was still throbbing and I could feel the sting of serum clear up to my neck. Instead of "Thank you," I said, "I hate Dr. Sams, I hate bunnies, I hate lollipops, and I hate you for bringing me here!" Pain gives you courage or maybe just the motivation to hurt others.

Mama didn't say anything. She just reached for Donna and held her steady while Dr. Sams reloaded and fired away on Donna's arm. While Donna flinched and cried, I watched Mama. She held Donna tight, but she was staring into space and tears were rolling down her face like little rain streams. Donna took her lollipop. It was red. Dr. Sams gave her mine too, but she wouldn't eat it until we were back in the car and I told her it was okay. There were other times I said or at least thought "I hate you," but the shot incident sticks in my mind.

Willene Wooten is pounding on the organ, "I Come to the Garden." I can feel every note shooting through my temples. Wish Donna was playing instead. Something happier like "Heart and Soul."

When Granny Crawford died and left us her piano, Mama signed us up for lessons. For me it was almost as bad as shots although I didn't hate Mama for piano lessons. What I did hate was sitting on that hard, cold piano bench for a solid hour every day. Mama said I should be able to play well, I had the hands for it. Then she would turn over a little hour glass she kept on the piano. I'd have rather counted the grains than practiced, but Donna was pretty good. I think she could have been professional if our piano teacher hadn't moved to Atlanta. Donna taught herself to play some pieces just by listening. She used to play for chapel at our elementary school back when it was okay to have chapel. She'd do hymns during the service but she always played "Blue Moon" to march in and "Heart and Soul" to march out.

Then there was tap dancing. Mama said it would make us "at ease socially." Daddy said it was a waste of time, and "Nobody tap dances through life, socially or otherwise." But he came to our recitals just the same. Mama took us every Saturday morning for lessons. That was after our piano teacher left town and I liked dancing better because I didn't have to sit still anymore — just shuffle tap, shuffle tap, heel toe, heel toe, and on and on until I felt like one of those little marionettes that came around to school once in a while and talked about tooth decay. Recitals were fun because we got to dress up in costumes — Siamese cats or valentines or poodles. Donna usually had a lead part, not that she was that good at tapping but she was so cute. When Mama fixed up Donna in her costume, she could put Shirley Temple to shame.

Blue, blue eyes and Q-tip dimples under a halo of blond curls waiting for a place to land. She looked like Little Miss Sunbeam. In fact, she won the Dixie store's Local Little Miss Sunbeam Contest. Aunt Kate said Donna could have made a living just tearing bread.

The best recital we ever had was the year we were poodles. This doesn't have anything to do with my feeling guilty about Mama. I just thought about it. I wonder if Donna remembers. Mama borrowed our teacher's pattern and made Donna's and my costumes. They were white and satiny with cotton balls glued around the edge of the skirts, like fringe, and around the wrists of the sleeves. Attached to the back of each skirt was a cord with a pompon on the end. Those were our tails. Aunt Kate said we looked more like snowflakes with tails than poodles. But our costumes were just like the picture on the pattern envelope and better than any of our classmates'.

Donna and Joanne McJunkin had the lead parts. Joanne was cute back then but not as cute as Donna. Lead part just meant they got to stand in front of the rest of us and do the same moves. The only difference came at the end. Donna and Joanne were supposed to curtsy to each other, turn, rub their little tail ends together, and tap off in opposite directions. It went well in rehearsal, but the night of the recital their tails wrapped around each other and the pompons knotted up. They didn't realize what had happened until they tried tapping off in opposite directions. Sort of a poodle tug of war developed. We all got to laughing in the background. Then the audience got into it. I could see Mama and Daddy. Mama looked embarrassed, Daddy just looked, but Aunt Kate was yelling, "Pull, Donna, pull!" Finally Joanne's tail ripped off taking a sizeable chunk of fabric with it. Then Donna lunged forward and disappeared behind the curtain. I was afraid she'd be embarrassed, but she heel-toed right back out on stage and curtsied to the audience.

I want to lean over to Donna and say "Nonna, remember the poodles?" Then break into giggles. It would be such a relief. I can almost picture Scarlet and Charlotte in our outfits.

Donna was the crowd pleaser all right and that suited me just fine. Except for one thing. That's the way she met Andrew. He

[55

was a judge for the Peach Festival beauty contest the year Donna was in it. The sponsors knew Crystabelle Dean was going to be in the pageant. Her family of wrestlers invented the grudge match if that tells you anything. The sponsors aimed for out-of-town judges. Yankees if possible. Donna won. When they called her name, her hands flew over her mouth and her knees buckled like she always did when she won a beauty contest. But she ended up with Andrew. She's still pretty and she still has Andrew. Aunt Kate calls that "irony of situation."

I was thinking about that beauty contest on the way home from the airport and wondering what if Donna had skipped Miss Peach Queen, not that I hate Andrew or anything. Just wondered if she couldn't have done more on her own, like being an airline stewardess or making commercials or being a beauty consultant for Maybelline. Jack tried to get her to do commericals for his dealership a few years back. All she'd have to do was point at a new Cadillac or Tornado or Cutless and say, "Jack Brighton treats you right!" But she wouldn't do it. Said she didn't have the confidence anymore. Still she was flattered to death and she told me so. I've missed Donna more than I ever thought. But she has the girls to fill her heart and occupy her time even if she does have to put up with Andrew.

I've missed Mama too. For the first time, I've started understanding that look in Mama's eyes, the distant look she got sometimes when she wasn't focused on anything in particular. I wondered if she loved Daddy, really loved him, if there'd ever been another man in her life. I wanted to sit down and ask her if she ever thought about leaving. And to hear her tell me, "Sarah, it's all right to feel that way — like you're floating and you can't get your feet to stick to the ground. All women feel it sometimes, even me."

I wish I could get back to where I was at Mimosa years ago, but I'm not sure I was ever really attached. More like an astronaut in a space capsule, grabbing whatever's nearby to keep from floating away. Like Mama, hanging on with all those projects.

God, I'm sweating. This dress must be made of rubber, black rubber, the stuff they make tires out of. It's smothering every pore in my body. I shouldn't complain. Donna went out and got it for me. But God! It's hot! How does Reverend Pierce stand that robe?

I feel like I'm floating in a pool of sweat. The humidity and all these people. Guess I got used to a different climate.

This past year I haven't felt so unattached either, not like I did here. I've been too busy collecting little bits of life, the kind you organize and put in a letter or give form and music and fit into a poem. Then it all makes sense.

Sometimes at the ranch where Michael and I stayed I'd go out and watch the blacksmith. He'd work his way around the horse, leg by leg, prying off the old shoe, clipping and trimming the bare hoof. He'd fire up a new shoe until it was red hot, hammer it on his anvil, then fit it to the hoof. Steam would shoot off but the horse wouldn't flinch. "No feeling there," he said. But it was still so hot that if he dropped it, it would set little bits of hay on fire. He'd stick the hot shoe sizzling into water, then nail it on the hoof.

I loved watching him work. The orange sparks, the steam, the ringing of the hammer against the anvil. He had a rhythm, almost a song. After he finished, the horses always looked so steady, so sure-footed like the shiny new metal gave them a firm hold on the ground, a place to leave a pattern like no one else's.

I kept thinking about that blacksmith on the flight home. Don't know why. That and Mama and how things like lame horses and beauty contests can change the course of your life. Andrew met me at the airport. I should have known Donna wouldn't drive if she could help it. Andrew's the same ole Andrew. I wasn't in the car five minutes before he started a lecture on the various stages of the female condition. I tuned him out and escaped into my own female condition. When he got to their house, Donna ran out and started hugging me almost before I was out of the car. Then we hugged and hugged some more just like we did as kids when we had a secret or a birthday or a trip to go on. For a few minutes I almost forgot the reason I'd come home. When I got to the hospital, I remembered.

Mama was white, bone white. Pale as she is right now. Her lips blended into her face. Her skin looked as thin as wrapping tissue and her hands like small translucent gloves. Daddy sat beside her. He looked up at Donna and me, not saying anything. Donna whispered something to him and they left the room. I sat beside Mama.

The chair still held Daddy's heat. I picked up her hand. I can feel it now, cool and light and so small, I'd never realized how small. Her nails were smooth and clear with little white moons. Her fingers draped into my palm like they were melted together except the little finger. It had its own direction. Mine's the same way, a crook in the little finger. Mama was proud of it, said we inherited it from her mother. But my hands aren't really like Mama's. She always called mine "artist's hands," because I have long thin fingers and an unbroken M in each palm. I never knew what the M was supposed to mean but Mama said it was special. Holding her hand, I kept looking for other connections but the little finger was all, a crooked little finger.

I tried to talk. To tell her why I left, to ask her how she'd been, to make her understand how sorry I was. She never opened her eyes or even moved. Finally I laid my head beside her shoulder and wept.

Mama died that night. The doctor said her heart just quit. Aunt Kate said it was for the best that the body goes when the heart does. Whatever that meant. She doesn't explain herself too often. But Lois Turpin agreed and got on the phone to everybody in the community. Then the people and the food started pouring in.

Donna and Daddy made arrangements with Mahoney funeral home. Mostly Donna. She had a time. Daddy insisted on putting this little stuffed dolphin Mama got at Sea World in her hands in the open casket. Donna told him people would think they'd gone crazy. She finally talked him into letting her put it at Mama's feet, "like it was swimming around down there."

Then Kate said, "Just have a closed casket. Viv wouldn't want people staring at her."

"They'll think she's all eat up with cancer," Donna said, "or withered away. And people like to pay their last respects. Andrew says you need to see the body to accept death and get on with your life."

So they left it open for the funeral home. Donna and Daddy stood next to the open end and Kate and I stood at the dolphin end. For two solid hours we listened to last respects. Funeral home visitation must be the closest thing in the civilized world to Indian rites of passage. A way of seeing how much the grieving family can endure to prove themselves worthy of the dead. "She looks so natural." "She's better off, you know." "Did you donate any organs?" I went home with Aunt Kate.

The farm felt welcome. Even in the dark, I recognized most of the ruts in the dirt driveway. Some felt larger. "Need to asphalt," Kate said, swaying the Blazer around the edge of the ruts like a barrel racer. We went in through the kitchen. Not much on the counters, a few letters, a book, an ashtray. I guess you could call it clean, as clean as I'd ever seen it, but more empty than clean. Before, there'd been jelly jars, cereal boxes, crackers, a loaf or two of bread, tea jug, telephone books, a clock in the shape of a horse's head, hand towels, at least two novels, and other bits and treasures filling in the cracks, all layered and pushed back on Aunt Kate's counters.

"What happened?" I asked.

Kate slid her keys the length of the counter. "Simplicity," she said.

"What?"

"I've simplified my life," she said. "You know, cleaned out, gotten rid of, molted like an old parrot." She disappeared behind the refrigerator door and reappeared with two cans. "Don't have any of that light stuff," she said. "You want a glass?"

I shook my head and we settled at the kitchen table. Kate popped her beer and lit a cigarette. "You know what gets me?" she said staring at the filter, "Clean living doesn't mean shit when it comes to dying. *Quelle merde, cette vie!* Pardon my French."

"Wish you could have seen her when we were growing up," Kate said. "She was so feminine, like Donna, only more fragile." She pulled on her beer. "Not that Viv was all that fragile, she just looked that way." Kate took another drink. "In a way," she said, "I was jealous." She turned the can up then made a grimace, a bitter smile. "I hate that last little bit. It always tastes like metal. You ready?" I shook my head and she disappeared behind the refrigerator door again.

"Why were you jealous?" I asked, watching Aunt Kate pop and light at the same time.

"Because Viv was so delicate-looking and there I was, sturdy as a fence post." She inhaled as though it was her last breath, then opened her mouth and let the smoke cloud around her face. She sat there not saying anything for a while. Just smoking and drinking like she was alone at a bar listening to a sad country song. "Funny thing is," she finally said, "she was stronger than me too. Not physically, but every other way."

"How?" I asked.

Kate stared into space, then back at me. "Did you ever see that picture of us?" Not waiting for an answer she stood up fast, swayed a little, then disappeared into the next room. When she came back, she cradled a small pewter frame in her hands as though it might break. She held it for me to see but didn't let go. In it stood Mama and Aunt Kate, barely in their teens. Mama was a little taller. Her light brown hair was long and pulled back. A fringe of curls framed her face and neck. Kate's hair was darker and in a bob. They both smiled. Mama's was more a hint of a smile, her mouth a tiny rosebud like Donna's. Kate's smile was broad, flirtatious.

"Both our dresses were white," Kate said, "but the photographer thought we needed color. He made Viv's blue 'to match your beautiful eyes' he said and mine soft yellow 'because you're warm as sunlight.' That's what he said." She laid the picture down and finished her beer. This time no grimace. "Say when," she shouted from the refrigerator.

Back again, she sat heavily at the table and lit another cigarette. The smoke began making me queasy but I wanted to hear more.

"Papa had the portrait made for Mother's Day. Wish Mama had been in it too, but it was a surprise for her. Right before she got sick. She loved it. But after she died, Papa couldn't look at it without crying. Viv and I kept it in the drawer."

I'd seen the picture a hundred times, but this time it looked different. The girls in the picture were so young. I closed my eyes and tried to imagine Mama and Aunt Kate riding horses, cracking pecans, telling secrets, grieving over their own mother. I wanted to be in the picture with them.

"To happier times!" Kate said, turning up her beer. "You haven't finished your first yet? Not a beer drinker anymore? What'd that vet do to you?"

"Not much taste for it tonight," I said. I wanted to talk about Mama, not Michael. "What did y'all do after your mother died?"

"Vivienne pretty much held the family together. We were barely in our teens and Papa was no help. I tried so hard to get his attention but he couldn't see beyond his own grief. Couldn't stand to come home without Mama there. He was no farmer anyway. Had to get sharecroppers to take care of the planting and livestock." Kate got this distant look in her eyes, and I swear it was the same as Mama's. It shot cold chills all over me.

"Your Mama was strong," she said. "She put things behind her and went on. I never could, but she did."

"What things?" I asked. Aunt Kate turned and looked me straight in the face.

"The past, Sarah. She let go of the past. She made a lot of sacrifices for you." "For her family," Kate added hurriedly.

I wasn't sure which family she meant, mine or hers, and Aunt Kate wasn't getting any clearer. She looked away from me, back into space and continued.

"But we managed." She lifted the photograph. "We took care of the house and ourselves well enough." She returned it to the desk drawer and got another beer.

"Did I tell you about Little Red?" she asked.

"Your setter-type dog?" I looked around for signs of Little Red and thought about my own Bilo.

" 'Type' is right. I called him my hybrid setter. He came up right after T.J. moved out."

"Who?"

"T.J. My boyfriend. He was here before you left. I think. Don't you remember him?"

"Yes," I lied. I had been so caught up in myself I hadn't noticed Aunt Kate's love life and to be honest it was too much to keep up with.

"Anyway, T.J. moved out and Little Red came up the same day. I wouldn't have taken him in, but he was just a puppy and he looked so lonely."

"So where is he?"

"Dead," she said, no change in expression. "I ought to be relieved. That damn dog cost me a fortune. First it was puppy shots, then worming, not just capsules but this $2-a-pill stuff you've got to cram down their throats every few weeks. Then distemper and rabies shots, neutering, flea dip." She was counting on her fingers and running out fast.

"Goddamn UPS truck!" Kate slammed both hands, palm down, against the table. The noise startled me. I felt its echo in the pit of my stomach.

"What?" I asked.

"The UPS truck ran over Little Red." She buried her face in her palms. "And it wasn't even my Goddamn package!" I'd never seen Kate cry before. But she was crying now, soft and low and as sad as I'd ever seen her. I helped her to bed. She didn't even fuss, just let me lead her like a sleepy child. Maybe I should have gotten drunk too. Instead I lay awake all night, thinking about mothers and sisters and little stray dogs.

This morning hasn't been any better. All these people crowded in the sanctuary. Jack's here. I didn't see him come in but I know he's behind me. You live with somebody that long, you don't have to see their feet to know where they're standing. I can feel his breath on the back of my neck. Hot like the rest of the church.

The smell of gardenias is stifling. But Mama always loved gardenias, their glossy green leaves and cotton white blossoms. Daddy has the place loaded with them. Donna couldn't stop him. Pretty, but the smell is nauseating like Aunt Kate's smoke last night.

Aunt Kate looks at me. Her eyes are red and puffy. "Are you all right?" she asks.

I nod but don't mean it.

Reverend Pierce finally starts. "Vivienne Crawford has overcome this world," he says, " . . . good mother . . . worked hard . . . loved her family . . . " His words come and go like a buzz saw. Now Donna looks at me, says something. Jack's breath burns my neck. The choir goes into "Amazing Grace, how sweet . . . "

I wake up, cooler, in the dark. I'm home. The whole room is black dark but I know where I am, unless I'm dreaming.

I've almost forgotten the feel of Jack's arms around me, his chin against my cheek, our bed. He holds me as though he could turn it all back in one night. Grief, love, sadness, and wild regret — all layered together and arced like a rainbow at my feet.

Jack makes love to me, while my mind shouts over and over, "Oh, Mama! What have I done?"

PART III

REUNION

JACK

Sarah is sleeping. I push back the hair from her forehead. She's still warm but not feverish like she was when I carried her in. I slip off her jacket and skirt. Then fold one side of the bed covers over her. I stretch out beside her, just to make sure her breathing stays normal. She doesn't seem to notice. She looks like she's taking an afternoon nap, the way she did sometimes when I'd come home for lunch. We'd end up in bed, then I'd leave her napping while I went back to work.

I want to say, "Why? Sarah? Why did you leave me? What did he do to make you stay away from me?" I feel tears thick behind my eyes. Our bedroom is quiet, too quiet, like it's been for over a year now.

I haven't slept here in a long time. I've spent most nights on the couch at the office. Eaten breakfast there too, if you want to call it that. I've had every flavor of Pop Tart there is. Nine in all, counting vanilla creme with chocolate glaze, which I don't like to think about. Ate them raw for awhile, then I took the toaster to the office. There are certain advantages to having your own business. Like sleeping there when you want to.

Guess this is the first time I stretched out on my own bed in six months or more. Feels good.

When Sarah left I stuck pretty close to home at first, thinking she might escape or call or something. After a while though, I just stayed at the office. The couch is short but I can sleep on my back with my feet hanging over. It's not too bad if you have a six-pack first. When I can't sleep, I go over inventories, sales figures, quotas. Caught a few errors. Guess the boys wish I'd go back home.

But hell, nothing there except Bilo. I wouldn't go at all if it weren't for him. But I keep thinking he might take off too.

I've eaten with Tommy some. Usually at Wayfarer or the Hungry Bull. All the waitresses know him. He says he quit cooking the day I left home.

I hadn't tried to talk to him much about Sarah. Except right at first when I thought she was kidnapped. He never brought her name up, not directly. He'd ask about business or Bilo or we'd talk about the Cowboys or Falcons — whoever's in season. Tommy's easy that way.

One night about two months ago we were at the Hungry Bull. Steaks hadn't come yet. We were still working on our salads. "Sweet tea?" a waitress asks, a pitcher in each hand. "You know it is," Tommy said, "just like you, Marlene." Marlene faked embarrassment, giggled, and poured tea out of the side of one pitcher without spilling a drop. Then she moved on to the next table.

"Tommy," I said, "why didn't you ever get married again after Brenda left?" Funny thing is, it never occurred to me until that moment of tea-pouring.

He didn't say anything for a minute. Just kept staring at a cherry tomato like it was part of the answer.

"I could of, I guess," he said, not looking up. "At first, anyway. There were plenty of girls who remembered me on the football field. That's what brought me and Brenda together, you know. She was a baton twirler. Gridiron was our common ground. But that was all. Excepting you."

He looked up. "She was a pretty little thing, I tell you, she was. Long brown hair, wavy like yours, and the cutest little figure you ever saw. Even after she had you, her waist went right back down. Didn't look like she even thought about having a baby." He laughed and looked back at the tomato. "Course I guess she really didn't think about it. Neither one of us did. We were too busy being teenagers.

"She could twirl a baton, though. Best one the high school's ever had, if you ask me. Nowadays a gal could probably get a scholarship twirling like that."

Marlene reappeared with our steaks. "I've got a medium-rare T and medium-well sirloin tips with peppers," she said, sliding the T-bone in front of Tommy. "Watch it, guys, the plates are sizzling."

Tommy speared the tomato and slid the salad bowl away. Marlene grabbed it and disappeared. Neither of us said anything for a couple of bites. Then Tommy spoke up again. "I just wish you could have seen her twirl that baton. She could throw it up so high you'd think it was gonna get caught in a cloud. It'd get small as a needle." He looked out across the restaurant like one might be sailing through. "Then the thing would arc and come falling down. But Brenda, she'd hold out one hand, the other behind her back, and catch it like it was just floating." Tommy looked back at me. "It sure was something."

"What happened to you and Brenda?" I asked. It was the first time I'd ever asked, man to man, and my voice shook a little.

"We were just kids," he said, lifting his knife. "A quarterback and a baton twirler. Take away our toys and we were lost." He cut a bite of T-bone. "That's why I never wanted you to depend on basketball too much," he said in between chews. "I was proud of you in high school, one proud daddy, but they were just games. I wanted you to have a real occupation when you got out of college. Not reliving some game all the time when you were a hero, you know, good memories that make you sad. Does that make sense?"

I nodded. He cut more steak. "As for Brenda, I blamed her a long time, but she tried. She tried playing wife and mama. A real husband and a real baby were too much for her, though. And she was still in love with the sky. Guess being an airline stewardess was like being that baton. She just never came back down, not to me anyway." Marlene reappeared with more tea. We both worked on our steaks a while.

Then Tommy swallowed hard, looked me right in the face and said, "She missed out on one hell of a fine son." He wiped his eyes with the back of his hand. My throat lumped up and I couldn't say anything for a minute. I just looked back and nodded.

"But hell!" Tommy said, his voice almost back to normal, "that's women for you. Some of them just don't never realize what they're missing!" He pushed his steak plate away and grabbed for the bill. I beat him to it. "Basketball players have quicker hands," I said. We both laughed, but inside I marveled at the strength of this man I'd known and not known all my life.

Now, looking at Sarah, I wonder if she's that much like Brenda. "What was it, Sarah?" I say out loud. "The sky? Drugs? That horse guy? Or just plain tired of me?" I lie there wishing I had Tommy's strength. At the same time I wonder what he'd have done if Brenda came back. Surely not all women are like this, I tell myself. Then I think about Joanne. Joanne McJunkin and the night I had with her.

She caught me one day coming through her checkout line at the Dixie store — "10 items or less." I mean, it doesn't take much for a man and a dog — a bag of Jim Dandy, suitcase of beer, few boxes of Pop Tarts, a can or two, some chips. I was going through Joanne's line like I always do because I never have over ten items, and she was friendly like she always is. "How's it going, Jack?" she said.

"It's going," I said.

She ran a can of spaghetti over the bar code sensor. No beep. She turned up her nose and ran it by again. "You shouldn't be eating this stuff," she said. "You need a real meal." Then all in the same breath she said, "Why don't I fix you one? Tomorrow night."

I didn't know what to say. I didn't even know her last name. I looked at her name tag. She had on a store smock like they all do but her name tag was right on the end of her left breast. I stared at it but I forgot to read it.

"Well?" she said in a little-girl voice. I looked at her face and she was smiling. A really sweet smile. I hadn't seen a woman smile like that in a long while. I looked at her name tag again and then back at her face.

She flipped her hair off the back of her neck and said, "I won't take 'no' for an answer." She wrote her address on the back of my receipt and dropped it into the bag. "See you around 7:00," she said.

I kept thinking about it all next day. Joanne McJunkin and dinner. I didn't even go over the inventory. I liked the idea of going and I didn't like it. I'd had it with women, if you know what I mean. If she'd written her phone number on the back of the receipt, I'd have called and canceled, told her we had a late shipment or something. But then I thought, what the hell! I could use a decent meal. Wonder what she looks like underneath that smock. I had the boys in service wash my car.

Before I knew it, I was standing at the front door of ll4 Chateau Apartments feeling like a fool. I rang once. The door eased open and there stood Joanne. She was wearing this red sweater. A long sweater or a short dress. I'm not up on women's fashions. Whatever it was, it was tight. She held two glasses of wine, a shade darker than her sweater. "Come in, Jack Brighton," she said, not in her little-girl voice this time. She stepped back.

Her living room was done in Mediterranean or Spanish, I'm not sure which. I never worked in a furniture store but I could find out. The whole set matched, even the TV console, Sears I'd guess. Dark wood with red fabric. Over the couch hung a pair of — I don't know if you'd call them prints or paintings. One was a matador with his cape straight out and a bull curving around behind him. The other was a dancing woman, her arms raised and castanets on her fingertips. Her skirt swirled out like the matador's cape exposing a pair of perfect thighs and frilly red panties. Both the matador and the dancer were on black velvet. They matched the decor.

"Nice apartment," I said.

"Thanks," she said, handing me a glass of wine. Little bits of something swirled around in it. "It's paid for, the furniture. Furman picked it out. And I paid for it. Can you believe that?" She swayed slightly and took a sip from her glass. "But I liked it too. Still do. It's lasted longer than Furman. Have a seat and I'll check on dinner."

"Who's Furman?" I called as she disappeared into the kitchen.

"My ex," she called back. She reappeared with a fresh bottle of Gallo. "Can you get the cork out of this thing? I'd rather have screw-off lids but when you get the best the Dixie store has to offer, you have to fool with a cork. I made a mess with the first one. Furman used to get the cork out."

"So tell me about Furman," I said, twisting the corkscrew straight down.

"Nothing much to tell," she said. "Met him at the Wayfarer, the lounge. He was driving for the Dixie store at the time, so we had something in common. We got married and saved up for him a rig of his own." She turned up her glass and finished the last sip. If her drink had cork crumbs she didn't seem to notice. "Then ole Furman drove away with my heart and kept going." She wiped her lips. "Guess he was in love, like the song says, with the white line."

The cork popped out and I poured Joanne another glass. "Not too much," she said after her glass was full. "Got to save room for dinner. You like lasagna?"

"Sounds good," I said, "and it smells good." She laughed. A sweet laugh. I did too.

"Then welcome to my table, Jack Brighton." She led me into the kitchen. It smelled like Pizza Hut. She slid two salad bowls from the refrigerator. "I tear the lettuce," she said, "so it won't get rusty. They say you can slice it if you're going to eat it the same day but I'd rather tear mine." She reached back in the refrigerator. "What kind of dressing you want?" She pulled three bottles, each a different color. "Take your pick. I grate my carrots too. Don't you just hate it when they give you those big chunks of carrots that you can hardly chew? Really ruins a romantic meal. I won't eat mine." She took a sip of wine. "Those cherry tomatoes are from California, but they're fresh. Just came in this morning."

"The salad looks really good," I said, shaking out a blob of Thousand Island. Joanne turned off the kitchen lights except the oven hood. She lit two candles and put them on the table. "Make a toast," she said.

"To a good dinner," I said lifting my glass.

"For a good man," Joanne added, looking from me to the candles and back to me. We both drank. It felt good.

By the end of the lasagna and the second bottle of wine, we pretty much covered the grocery business and world of automobile sales. Joanne produced another bottle of wine. It had a screw-on cap. "Didn't think we'd do in both bottles of Gallo," she said, giggling a little. "This is my spare. It's white but I guess it's okay to mix colors."

"Guess so," I said, pushing back from the table but not ready to leave.

She wrung off the lid and refilled our glasses. It mixed with the last of the red in each glass and turned pink, pale like pink champagne. "Follow me," Joanne said, leading me back into the living room. I sat on her couch underneath the matador and castanet player with the swirling skirt.

"How do you stay in such great shape?" Joanne asked, sitting beside me, almost touching.

"I'm not, not like I used to be," I said.

"Bet you played sports," she said, leaning closer. "Basketball? You're tall enough!"

I nodded.

"I was a cheerleader," she said, "Made the uniform myself, royal blue and canary yellow. The skirt had little box pleats that kicked out when we jumped." She smiled that really sweet smile again and I could almost see her in one of those little short skirts, legs like the castanet player, jumping up and down in front of crowded bleachers.

"Still have it," she said, "packed away in my hope, uh, cedar chest. Right underneath the silverware I got for my wedding. Four forks, three knives, seven spoons, and a serving fork. It's sterling. Never got the complete set." She stared at her pink wine. Then she looked up, smiling again, but not the same. "Tell me about your basketball days."

"Nothing much to tell," I said, and before I knew it I was reliving my entire memory of close games, bad calls, tournaments, and scholarship offers. I couldn't believe how interested Joanne was. I even promised to dig out my old scrapbook of press clippings and let her see them. She seemed pleased.

"We need some music," Joanne said, "some classic rock." She jumped up, steadied herself with one hand on my shoulder, and walked over to a huge stack of album covers. Then she collapsed on the carpet and folded her legs, Indian style. "I've got the Beatles, the Stones, Neil Diamond, Johnny Rivers, mystery music, and a whole lot more. Good ole 33-and-a-thirds. Request line is open, Jack Brighton," she said, smiling up at me.

"Surprise me," I said. She closed her eyes, chose four albums, and pulled out the records without looking at the covers. Then she opened her eyes and dropped them on the turntable.

"I'll surprise us both," she said, easing back onto the couch beside me, this time closer. Her thigh touched mine.

The first album dropped. The song was vaguely familiar — "magic moment . . . sweeter than wine." I couldn't believe I was listening to the lyrics. Sarah always did. If she liked a song, she could just about quote it, word for word. I never paid that much attention. She'd say, "How can you like a song if you don't know what it's saying?"

"Know who that is?" Joanne said, interrupting my thoughts. I didn't answer. "Jay and the Americans." She shifted slightly. Her skirt caught on my thigh and slipped up a little. The song was soft and sweet. I put my arm around Joanne and touched her hair. Bright blonde but softer than it looked. She leaned against my chest. We stayed that way through two more songs, both love songs. Then I reached around with my other arm and pulled her to me. She slipped her arm around my back and laid her head against my chest. I couldn't believe how good it felt to hold a woman, smell her perfume, feel her arms around me. It'd been so long.

Too long. I didn't even care about kissing her, not yet, I just wanted to hold her and to be held.

I'd still be there if it wasn't for the next album. It was a woman singer, a screamer. As good as it felt to hold Joanne, I kept getting distracted by that voice. "Who is that?" I asked Joanne, straightening up a little. "I know I've heard her. I think I've even seen her."

"Janis Joplin," she said. "Remember her group, Big Brother and The Holding Company?"

Something stirred in my memory, like pieces of a bad dream. I could see her on stage. The voice kept screaming.

"Her album's 'Cheap Thrills,'" Joanne said, pulling me closer. "She's dead now."

The singer went into "Break it . . . another little piece of my heart" and it hit me like a bolt. I felt a rush of emotions I could barely hold back. I stood straight up. "I've got to go," I told Joanne.

What I couldn't tell her is that the other time I heard Janis Joplin was at a jam or concert — or whatever the hell you want to call it — with Sarah, on our honeymoon.

I look at Sarah, still sleeping. "Damn you, Sarah!" I say out loud. "You screwed my life up without even being here."

I meant to call Joanne the next day, apologize, and ask her out for dinner. But that was the same night Sarah's mother died. I didn't even know she was sick! I'd quit going over to the Crawfords' after Sarah left, but Donna Jean should have called. Of course, I don't put a whole lot of stock in what she says. If she had told me her mother was deathly ill, I'd have taken it for a bad cold. Donna Jean's still cute-looking but dingy, one hundred percent. And quite a talker. Half the time about nothing, like what's going on at the beauty shop or who she read about in one of those grocery-store newspapers. Don't know how Andrew stands it. Sarah says the same thing about Andrew and Donna, only the other way around.

The whole family babies Donna Jean to death, Sarah included. They should have named her Prima Donna Jean. When she had the twins you'd have thought she died and came back to life. And Andrew made like he delivered them. The way the Crawfords carried on, I don't see how Sarah stood it. She'd already lost two.

And all she'd heard from her family was "It was probably for the best" or "You can always try again." And there was Donna with one she expected and one she didn't. Sarah lost so many.

Lying here, she looks like she did in the hospital after she lost the first baby, so thin and frail and tired. Maybe that's it! Maybe she's been too weak to leave. Or brainwashed! Like with Patty Hearst where the victim identifies with the captor. And maybe it took her mother's death to snap her out of it. Or maybe it was just a guilty conscience.

I heard about Mrs. Crawford the morning after she died. "Heard" nothing, I read it in the paper. How do you like that? I'm in the family for twenty years, then I have to read about my own mother-in-law's death in the newspaper. Vivienne was the closest thing to a mother I ever had. I should have at least gone to see her. By the time of the funeral I was feeling all kinds of emotions — guilt, sadness, regret, and anger, anger mostly at Sarah.

But I wasn't prepared when I saw her this afternoon at the funeral. Sarah was thinner, eight pounds at least, and she looked strung out. That's when I started thinking again that she might be on something. When she fainted, I was almost convinced. I carried her out by myself. Had to. Mr. Crawford was too grief-stricken to notice and Andrew looked like he was about to pass out too. I just scooped her up in my arms. The church was packed but I elbowed my way through the crowd. Then I drove straight here. The whole time I could hear Janis Joplin screaming in my head, "Take another . . . piece of my heart . . . "

Carrying her like that, all limp and helpless, reminded me of our honeymoon. I had an uncle in Palm Beach, Tommy's brother. He didn't come to the wedding, but he offered Sarah and me a place to stay for the weekend. I'd planned for us to go to a big auto race down there, but it was the wrong weekend and there was a rock concert instead.

Sarah wasn't nearly as disappointed as I was about missing the race. She begged me to go to the concert. My uncle called it a love-in. It was more a smoke-in. Throughout the day and half the night all kinds of groups performed, names I can't remember now. Most have split up or died since. But there was this one singer, a gal of about twenty, I can still see and hear her in my mind. Her singing was more wailing or mournful screaming than anything I've ever heard. She was wild — her hair, songs, voice, antics everything about her. Janis Joplin. I'd forgotten her name until the other night at Joanne's. I remember her more than the other performers because of the wild sadness in her voice and because Sarah kept singing her words.

On the day of the concert my eyes were still recovering from oats Kate threw at the wedding, and after hours — about eight — of looking through a sea of smoke I was almost blind. I told Sarah I had to get some air and left her for a while. It was a mistake. All day long the joints had come by, one right after the other. I just passed them on. Now I don't mind some wine or beer or smooth bourbon, but I'm not into killing my brain through my lungs. Never was. But while I was gone, Sarah took her turn, mine too evidently, because when I got back she was walking around in circles, stepping high like she was in briars.

She said she couldn't get her feet down and she kept yelling "Take another little piece of my heart!" She finally passed out. I could have strangled her, then and there. At the same time I would have fought anybody and anything to protect her. That's the way I felt at the funeral, too.

Sarah moves. It's almost dark. I must have dozed off too. "Sarah," I whisper, "are you okay?"

She doesn't say anything. She just looks at me. Those green eyes I thought I'd never see again.

My throat tightens but I say, "You're home."

She pushes her hair back from her neck. "I know," she says.

"I'll get you some water," I say and start to get up. But she catches my arm.

"Hold me," she says. "Please, just hold me for a little while." Before I can think, my arms go around her, pull her to me. I feel her hair underneath my chin, soft against my neck. The control I've worked on for so long explodes and a whole year's emotions come falling down on me. She clings to me like she's drowning. It's like we're both drowning. And I'm not sure if we're saving each other or pulling each other down. We make love, desperate love. A year's worth of passion rips me apart.

The next morning I wake up in Sarah's arms. I want to stay in bed, start over, but I have to clear my head. I don't want to wake her until I have control of myself. So I slip out of her arms, pull the sheet back over her, and dress quietly.

Breakfast. We'll need breakfast. Then we can talk. I head out for the Dixie store. Eggs, bacon, bread, butter, milk, grapefruit. I've got coffee at home but I remember tea. Sarah always loved hot tea, the expensive kind in little tea bags like Earl Grey. I throw in a box. I reach for a jar of orange marmalade. She used to like that too. Before I know it, I'm going through Joanne McJunkin's checkout line. I should have avoided her and would have if I hadn't been so wrapped up in my thoughts of Sarah.

"Morning, Jack Brighton," she says, with that sweet smile, but watching me closely. "You're out awfully early this morning."

"Yes," I say, feeling kind of guilty, "guess I am."

She fluffs her hair back from her ears. Then she starts sliding my groceries across the bar scan. She's slow, slower than I've ever seen her, turning each item two or three times like she's studying it or can't find the bar code. She reaches for the silver tea box. "Earl Grey?" she says. "I never figured you for a hot tea drinker."

"I'm not," I say. "It's for — for someone else."

Joanne's smile disappears. She doesn't look me in the face again. "That'll be $12.58," she says, stuffing everything into one bag. At that moment I hate myself. And I hate Sarah. Damn it! She's screwing up lives of people not even kin to her! I plan to say that to her, too. To tell her what she's done. Right after we finish breakfast. And if I'm sure she's not drugged or brainwashed.

When I get home, Sarah's already up. She's wearing one of my shirts. She's sitting on the kitchen floor, playing with Bilo. My throat lumps up again and I want to fall all over the two of them, to hug them long and hard. But I keep control.

"Good morning," she says, looking up but not directly at me. "Hope you don't mind." She pulls at the shirt. "Couldn't put that black suit back on. Synthetic. Hot as blazes. Nice of Donna to get it, but I hope I never wear it again." She goes back to playing with Bilo. "I think he's grown some," she says.

"He was full grown when you left," I say. She doesn't answer. "Got some breakfast stuff, here," I say, sliding the bag on the table. She starts to get up. "No, I'll cook." I look into the grocery bag. "You catch up with Bilo. He's probably missed you." She still doesn't say anything. I reach for the eggs and notice they're on top of the bread. So are the grapefruit. I wonder if Joanne realized the way she packed.

I cook the bacon in a frying pan, like Tommy always did. Sarah used to microwave it, but it gets too hard and crunchy that way. At least for me. I twist the oven knob to broil and slide in a pan of bread slices. Toaster's still at the office. Then I beat five eggs — three for me, one for Sarah, one for Bilo. He's gotten used to having breakfast with me. Likes eggs and bacon better than Pop Tarts, but he'll eat whatever I give him.

I don't fool with grits. Never did like them. Andrew and I have that in common, that and being married to two Crawford women. That's enough.

Sarah's watching me so I say, "You can do the grapefruit." I fix two plates and Bilo's bowl. I keep it under the table. Then I fix a cup of coffee for me and tea for Sarah. The whole time I'm thinking what all I'm going to say to her after breakfast. But I'm having trouble figuring it out. She gets the grapefruit done and we sit down to eat. I don't ask a blessing or say grace or anything. Haven't in over a year. For some reason Joe's blessing runs through my head.

"Thanks for the tea," she says, wrapping her hands around the cup.

"You're welcome," I say with flashbacks of Joanne's face at the Dixie store. We start eating, and the meal goes pretty well until I say, "Haven't had grapefruit in a while." Sarah stares at her half of grapefruit like she doesn't know what it is. Then she starts crying. Quiet-like at first, then higher and higher and louder until she's shaking with these high-pitched mournful sobs. I don't know what to say or do. I've never seen her like this. In twenty years of marriage I've hardly seen her cry at all. She always said she looks ugly when she cries. Sitting there watching her, I have to agree. But she also looks like a lost child. She may not be drugged or brainwashed but something's sure wrong with her. Our talk, I decide, will have to wait. I get up, go to her, and hold her again.

SARAH

"**S**it where you want to," Donna says, holding a platter of roast beef close against her like it might get away. We all sit where we've sat for the past four Sundays. Daddy on one end, the chair at the other end nearest the kitchen left for Donna, Andrew on the side next to Donna, Charlotte and Scarlet beside him, and Aunt Kate, Jack, and me across from them. A full table. Donna and Andrew's table. Their dining room furniture is finished in antique white with deep pink cushions in the chairs. A huge arrangement of silk geraniums sits on the sideboard. The room has a garden-like look. A real switch from Mama's mahogany.

The first Sunday dinner without Mama was the hardest, but Donna insisted on us eating together "for Daddy" she said. She moved it to her house. "Smart idea," Jack said. It surprised us both. His saying "smart" in connection with Donna.

"Daddy, will you say grace," Donna says more than asks. She sets the roast in front of him.

"Let Jack do it," Daddy says staring at the meat. Some slices are black, others are red.

Jack hesitates. I wonder if he's forgotten the words. Andrew glances at Donna but she's not looking. Then Jack says, "Bless this food to the nourishment of our bodies, amen."

"Y'all start on the meat," Donna says heading into the kitchen. "I'll get the rice."

"Can I help?" I call after her. Jack looks at me but doesn't say anything.

"You get the corn," Donna shouts over her shoulder, "and the string beans."

I slip back from the table. Jack holds onto my chair and gives my elbow a little lift as though I'm too weak to stand by myself. What's he thinking? I wonder.

I've wondered that over and over since I've been home. Since the morning after Mama's funeral when I woke up in our bedroom.

Jack was already standing, facing away from me. A wedge of sunlight slipped around the corner of the window shade and landed on his back. He's thinner, I noticed, and that little roll around his waist is gone. The hair on his back looked gold in the sunlight. I was always amazed that a brunette could have that fuzzy light hair on his back, but Jack did. Michael was darker than Jack, yet his back was smooth, almost hairless. It didn't make sense.

I pretended to be asleep but I watched Jack get dressed, as though I hadn't seen him dress a thousand times before. He pulled on his boxers, then stepped into his khakis. Michael didn't wear underwear. Said he didn't need it unless it was cold. Then he wore long johns, the thermal kind. Jack buttoned a striped shirt and slipped on his loafers. No socks. For some reason that seemed funny and I wanted to laugh. He turned toward me as though he heard my thoughts. I closed my eyes tight. He stood there about ten seconds more, then walked out. In a few minutes I heard him drive away.

I got up, found one of Jack's shirts thrown up on the dresser, and wrapped myself in it. It was deep red with tiny green lines crisscrossing all through it. One I'd bought a few years back. I was surprised he still wore it.

I wasn't hungry but thought I'd better try something, maybe toast. I checked the bread box. A crumpled bag with two moldy heels. I'd forgotten about bread mold. Things didn't mold so easily in Texas. You could leave a box of Saltines open for a week and they wouldn't even get floppy. Nothing in the cupboard except some canned spaghetti and a bag of chips, opened. I was almost afraid to look in the refrigerator. With good reason. Sour milk, slick lettuce, black tomato juice, and all kinds of beer. Probably whatever brand was on special at the time. Jack's not cheap but he gets fascinated when he sees those discount signs that say "REGU-LAR PRICE $6.50, SALE PRICE $5.99." He goes over to the display, figures out the price per can, then cents per ounce, then decides he'll try it while it's on special. Anyway, looks like he'd tried a lot of specials lately.

I gave up on food when I heard scratching at the kitchen door. "Bilo!" I shouted, opening the door. If dogs can look surprised, he did. I sat down in the middle of the floor, threw my arms around him, and cried like a baby. I was glad Jack wasn't there to see me. I was still hugging Bilo when he came back but I wasn't crying anymore. He was carrying a bulging grocery bag. He gave the door a backward kick and set the bag on the table. Then he moved quickly unloading eggs, bacon, grapefruit, bread, and some other things I couldn't see.

I'm still thinking about our own kitchen as I walk into Donna's.

"Hope the rice isn't sticky," Donna says.

"What?" I say.

"The rice, hope it's not sticky. You know Mama's never was." She hands me a bowl of corn and a bowl of green beans. Mama's good china bowls.

"Hers was sticky sometimes," I say, "but yours isn't." Donna smiles pretty enough for a photogragh. She picks up the bowl of rice and the gravy boat and we head back into the dining room. Donna sets the rice and gravy in front of Andrew. He stares at the gravy boat like it may be dangerous.

"Help yourself to whatever's in front of you," Donna says, "and pass it on."

I take a little corn and hand the bowl to Jack.

He looks me in the face. "You need more than that," he says. His eyes are soft and blue.

We didn't look each other in the face, not right away, the morning after the funeral. Jack unloaded the groceries and started cooking the bacon. He used the heavy black skillet Mama gave us for our first anniversary. I always microwaved bacon but Jack fried it, turning and smashing the strips like they were snakes about to attack. Then he filled a cookie sheet with bread slices, spread them with margarine, and broiled them in the oven. I looked for the toaster. It was gone. I shot a quick glance in the direction of the microwave. It was still there.

Jack beat and punched the eggs into shape while I fixed the grapefruit. I hadn't had grapefruit in over a year. But now it seemed like I hadn't missed a morning. Automatically, I went for the pointy spoons in the silverware drawer. They were pushed way back, cradled one in the other. Looking at those spoons, I almost cried. But I didn't, at least not then. I put them on the table and sat down. My foot scraped against something. Bilo's bowl. Jack had always made me feed Bilo outside. I wondered about the change. Jack set our plates down, reached under the table for the bowl, and filled it with a third of the eggs. Then he threw in a slice of bacon and a piece of toast.

"He's my buddy," Jack said, a little defensively.

"Should I fix him grapefruit, too?" I asked.

Jack laughed. Looked me in the face for the first time all morning and laughed again. Then cleared his throat and said, "Let's eat."

I made myself eat a little of everything on my plate even though the bacon was as chewy as Donna's roast beef. But when I tried to spoon out a wedge of grapefruit, I began thinking about Jack and Mama and Bilo and little pointy spoons. The tears started pouring. I didn't want Jack to see me cry. I tried to get up, but Bilo was woven around my legs, licking my toes like he was looking for fleas. I hid my face in my hands. Before I could shake free, Jack came to me, pressed his palms around my cheeks, and looked me straight in the face. Then he kissed me on the forehead. Like a father. Like Daddy never did.

Daddy doesn't even talk to me anymore. Not to anybody much. I think it's from grief over Mama, but Donna says it's from having his routine upset. I look at him now. He's staring in his plate, his hands flat on the table.

"Y'all won't believe this," Donna says forking a piece of roast. "What I heard at Holly's Hair and Then Some."

"You talking about two-tone Holly?" Aunt Kate asks.

"Two-tone Holly?" Andrew says. "Is her hair a variety of shades?" He chooses the smallest slice of roast beef left on the platter.

"Two-tone suntan," Aunt Kate says. "She only sunbathes on one side."

"Which side?" Scarlet asks, passing the roast without taking any.

"Lying on her back," Kate says. She presses little grains of rice into her fork as she talks. "Holly's real tan on the front, but her back's as white as a fish's belly."

"Maybe it's an abnormal fear of being unprotected," Andrew says, sawing on his piece of roast. "An instinctive sort of impulse for survival."

"No," Donna says, "Holly said she doesn't have time to lay on both sides." She looks around the table. "Anyway, she won't be two-tone any more. Oh sakes! I forgot the rolls." Donna jumps up and runs into the kitchen. "Hope they're still warm," she says when she comes back. She sets them in front of the twins. Charlotte grabs one. The first thing I've seen go on her plate.

"Why?" Andrew says, still sawing.

"So the butter will melt." Donna passes the rolls.

Andrew's face twitches. "Not the rolls! Why won't Holly be two tones anymore?" He stresses each word like he's hammering nails. Jack nudges me with his knee.

"Because she bought a tanning bed," Donna says, patting Andrew's arm. "Set it up in her shop so she can rent out times for people to come in and use it. But that's not what I started to tell about, what happened at the beauty shop. Scarlet, honey, hand Daddy a roll. Need some butter, Daddy?"

Daddy nods.

"So what did happen?" Jack asks.

"It wasn't actually at the shop but near it. There was this wreck just right up the road a ways from Holly's Hair and Then Some. Up near Tom's Quick Stop. Only it wasn't exactly a wreck."

"What exactly was it?" Andrew asks. A little piece of roast breaks loose and he loads it onto his fork.

"It was several things," Donna says. "You need a roll, Sarah?" She pushes the bread basket toward me. "This couple, I don't know if they were married or not. Anyway, they went out for milk — that's what they told the police, 'milk' — and they ran out of gas. It was 9:30 in the morning. Holly said she'd just put her first customer under the dryer — I think it was Wilene — when they heard the fire truck."

"You said they gave out of gas," Andrews says between chews.

"They did," Donna says. Even Daddy's starting to look interested. "But when they gave out of gas, the car caught on fire. Aunt Kate, you need some more tea. Anybody need anything while I'm up? Andrew?" Andrew doesn't say anything. His hand is on his jaw. He's still chewing. Kate is holding her piece of roast with her fingers and biting it like it's beef jerky. Donna returns with the tea pitcher.

"What kind was it?" Jack asks.

"A car fire," Donna says. "Are there different kinds?"

Jack looks at me. "Did anybody get hurt?" I ask.

"No," Donna says, "but the man got arrested."

"For what?" Daddy says. He startles me.

[81

"For being," Donna lowers her voice, "buck nekkid."

"He wasn't wearing anything?" Scarlet asks.

"According to Holly, not a stitch but a sock."

Aunt Kate lays down her piece of meat and says, "Where was the sock?"

Donna glances at the twins. Charlotte is staring at her plate, but Scarlet is staring straight at Donna.

"On his foot," Donna says, jumping up from the table. "I'm not sure which. I'd better get the pie."

Donna brings out two pies, both peach, and everybody has a piece. She's better at desserts. Aunt Kate asks for ice cream on hers and Jack has a second slice. Watching them all — Donna, the twins, Daddy, Aunt Kate, even Andrew — I can't believe how much I've missed Sunday dinners.

Jack and I laugh on the way home mostly about Donna's stories and Andrew's twitches. It feels good to laugh with Jack, almost normal. When we get home, Bilo runs to greet us.

"Why don't you take a nap?" Jack says.

"I could use one," I say, wondering if Jack plans to join me.

I slip out of my dress and under the comforter. The bedroom is cool. Blue and cool. I used to think about painting it yellow in the winter, for warmth, and back to blue in the summer. Jack said I'd end up with a green mess. He worked in a paint store when he was in high school so I guess he knows. Anyway, blue's just fine right now. And I'll be gone before winter.

I listen for Jack. The newspaper. I hear him turning pages. I keep listening.

Something about the way a house sounds. Water pipes popping, the freezer fan coming on and going off, wind whining through the screen porch. I hadn't thought about the sounds in this house for a year or more, but now they seem louder, more distinct. Like cicadas or tree frogs on a summer night, singing in the background. You don't notice them that much until there's a lull in the conversation or you're trying to sleep. Then you hear them almost like it's your brain running, humming while you try to think of something to say or drift off to sleep. That's when I hear the house sounds.

I never did like this house. It's a terrible thing to say, I know. And I can just hear Mama, "Now Sarah, think of all the homeless who would give anything, if they had anything, for a house like yours." Mothers don't have to be alive to make you feel guilty. But this past year I've begun being honest with myself. More honest than I ever was when I acted daughterly or wifely or "in the realm of normality," as Andrew would say.

As for our house, I wanted a wooden one that had an upstairs, something like Aunt Kate's. Jack wanted one story. "More heat efficient," he said, and brick, "less maintenance." That's what we have, what the contractor called a ranch provincial. But there's nothing ranchy about it. Unless you consider the fireplace, the only part I like. But Jack wouldn't use it. "Eighty percent of the heat goes straight up the chimney," he always said, "and Duke Power gets a bonus." In the winter I used to build a blazing fire every time he was out of town. But I'd turn off all the lights to save power.

For a while last year, Michael and I stayed with some friends in Tennessee. Annie and Russell. Russell was a carpenter and Annie was a weaver. They had the most wonderful house. Slabside on the outside and paneling on the inside. All pine. Russell said he got the boards from a nearby sawmill. The ceiling went up to a point like a circus tent. And a huge stone fireplace reached through the center.

There was a little loft with room enough for one low bed. You had to climb a ladder to reach it. It made me think of an indoor tree house. The kitchen cabinets were pine, "rough hewn" Michael called it. Russell made the dinner table out of a broad slab of black walnut. It was smooth as Mama's mahogany. Annie used a wood stove to cook on. The house seemed alive. The smells and textures. It was like living in a work of art. I loved being there.

Michael and I talked about staying in the Tennessee mountains, building our own house. We used to lie in bed, mapping out the house in our imagination. I wanted a little stained glass window over the bathtub, red roses with green leaves and amber between the flowers. Michael wanted beams where he could hang his guns and fishing gear. And a fireplace so big you could walk into it. He said we'd have a platform bed. He'd build it himself. Goose feather mattress but no springs.

Annie and Russell's beds were low, practically on the floor, and Annie had woven covers for each one. Michael and I slept in the loft. It was warm and cozy and I could practically touch the stone fireplace with my toes. It's the first bed I really liked since the one Jack and I slept in at Mimosa.

[83

No telling what Jack paid for this one. He read three or four consumer-guide books before he bought it. I'd still choose that half-shot bed at Mimosa Trailer Park. Guess I'm as crazy as Andrew thinks. Maybe it was the rainbow more than the bed. I almost drift off to sleep thinking about those Mimosa days.

The mattress shifts, startles me. Jack is sitting beside me. "You awake?" he whispers.

"No," I whisper back. "I'm talking in my sleep." I touch his hand.

He doesn't seem to notice. "Think I'll go over to Tommy's and watch the game," he says.

"Oh," I say, and move my hand.

"Feeling okay?"

"Yes," I say, turning on my side.

"Then I'll see you when I get back." The mattress shifts again as he stands. "Call me if you need me," he says over his shoulder. I watch him walk away.

I try to fall asleep but my mind won't let me. I wonder if Jack's had a girlfriend. If he has one now. Not that it's any of my business. But I keep looking for signs like a pink toothbrush or curling wand or bath powder. A year's a long time for a man like Jack, any man, to go without. I'm not about to ask him. I did ask Donna, though, and she said she hadn't seen him enough to know. She said somebody at Holly's mentioned Joanne McJunkin. But her name always comes up when there's a man on the loose. If Jack does have a girlfriend, she isn't much of a cleaner. Not around the molding where dog hair and year-old dust are thick as the carpet.

"Maybe he's over there now," I think out loud, "at his girl-friend's instead of Tommy's." I pick up the phone. I can't remember Tommy's number. I hang it back up. It's his business, I tell myself, and if he does have a girlfriend, I'll feel less guilty.

Sunday dinner with the family, the newspaper, watching the game at Tommy's, taking a nap. Amazing, how fast you can get back into a routine even when you think you're making fresh choices every day. Reminds me of a horse at the ranch, a filly named Dijon. I noticed her the first day she came to the ranch. We hadn't been there long and I was fascinated with each new herd of horses they brought in. Dijon stood out. She was Athene's size but her coloring was different — really unusual — buckskin with a stripe, a shade darker, running from her withers along her backbone to the base of her tail. "Dun stripe," Michael called it. "Adds $400 or $500 to her value. A fine looking filly."

But the next evening he sounded different. "That filly's got the worse case of head-shy I've ever seen," he said, dusting off horse hair. "We couldn't even get a halter on her. Had to lock her in a head gate just to worm her." He looked at me for understanding, those dark eyes. I nodded. "She was shaking so bad when we finished," he said, rolling up his sleeves, "I was afraid she'd founder." He washed from his finger tips to his elbows and kept talking about Dijon. He went back out three or four times that night to check on her.

Michael's like that. Especially about horses. I've seen him break down and cry when a customer's horse had to be put to sleep and furious at another customer for leaving a halter on a mare. "Never, never, never leave on a halter!" he shouted. "She'll scratch her ear with her hind foot, get it caught, and end up breaking her damn neck!"

He was back out the next morning checking on Dijon before I got up. "Sarah! Wake up!" He pounded the bed on both sides of me. "What?" I screamed, sat straight up, and banged into his forehead. He acted like he didn't feel it. "The trainer's out there with that crazy filly. He claims he can have her shy-broke, saddle-broke, and ready for a trail ride by mid-afternoon." He threw me some jeans and a shirt. "This, we've got to see."

I'd barely dressed and grabbed a piece of toast before Michael was pulling me out the door. My forehead still hurt. But I forgot about it when we reached the training pen. It was round, about forty or fifty feet across — Jack would know exactly if he saw it — and the sides were tall without much space between the slats. The trainer stood in the center. He was small, no taller than me. His hat looked two sizes too big. He held a coiled rope, the coils in his right hand and the end of the rope in his left. He nodded at us. Dijon eyed him from across the ring. The morning sun shimmered off her back and and the curve of her neck. She was beautiful. And she was scared.

Pete, the blacksmith, was watching too. "Never get tired of seeing ole Norris work the round pen," he said. "Best trainer we've had." He spit on the ground. "Sorry," he said to me. Then to Michael, "His work makes my job a lot easier."

"But in less than a day?" Michael said.

"Half a day," Pete said, "if he doesn't have an audience." He looked at me again and winked. "Likes to show out a little."

Michael slipped his arm around me, pulled me toward him. "We'll see," he said.

Norris clucked at Dijon, more a cross between a cluck and a whistle. She perked her ears. He waved the coiled rope. She backed flat against the fence.

Then Norris clucked, lunged, and threw the coil of rope at her rump. Dijon took off running against the edge of the pen, circling Norris again and again. He moved in a tiny circle always facing her, drawing in the rope, coiling it, and throwing it again if she slowed down. "Can't train a horse that doesn't move," he shouted in our direction. "Now we can start."

The first thing he taught her was simply to reverse to the outside and run the other way. He'd take two steps toward her, cluck, and throw the rope at her front quarters. She'd stop, face the fence, spin around on her hind legs, and begin another circle. After that, he taught her to turn to the inside. He'd take a step back and throw the rope in front of her. If she turned to the outside, he'd throw the rope in front of her again. Back and forth, back and forth, like he was cutting cattle. She looked confused and frightened but she finally turned to the inside. He threw the rope behind her and let her run more circles. This went on until Dijon made all the turns the way Norris wanted her to.

"She's learning to make the right choices," he shouted. "Now I'll teach her to come to me." He let her stop running. She'd begun to lather. Steam rose from her back. But instead of calling her name or walking toward her, Norris made the same clucking noise that meant run. Dijon tensed. Then he waved the rope and she took off again. He let her run, but each time she stopped, he clucked to her. If she looked at him, he'd wait a few seconds before he'd make her run. Then he'd wave the rope and she'd take off. But she ran less and less and watched him more and more.

"She's tired of running circles," Norris shouted to us. "Now she's trying to decide how to avoid it." He waved the rope and she walked several steps around the edge of the fence, never taking her eyes off him. He clucked again. Instead of moving around the circle, she turned straight toward the trainer. She lowered her head and took a step. Then another.

"I'll be damned," Michael said. "She's going to him." But she stopped about ten feet before she reached him.

Norris clucked again, let her stand there a few seconds more, then threw his rope and sent her running. This time she ran less than half the circle. He clucked. She turned, took a step toward him, then another and another like she was walking on slippery ground. But she didn't stop until she reached Norris in the center of the pen. Her ribs shot out with each breath. He spoke to her softly and reached to rub her forehead. She jerked her head away but didn't run.

The blacksmith looked at Michael. "Well?" he said.

"He's good," Michael said, "but she's still head-shy."

Pete laughed. "That's next."

Norris took the coiled rope and rubbed it against Dijon's neck. She bobbed her head but didn't move her feet. Then he ran the coil across her back, against her sides, up her chest, back to her neck.

She soon stopped bobbing her head. But instead of stroking her forehead like I thought he would, he waved the rope in her face. She shied, took several steps back, but she didn't run. He jumped at her, threw up his hands, waved again. She backed away. Norris turned and walked toward the center of the ring. Dijon followed. Then he whirled around shooing and waving like he was trying to run off a stray dog. She jerked her head back but didn't move her body. Sweat rolled down her neck in dark streaks. Finally, Norris reached out, rubbed her forehead. She didn't shy. He laid the rope coil over her ears like a crown. He turned and took several steps away from her. She followed. He turned and rubbed her head again.

Then he walked to the fence where Michael and I were standing, Dijon right behind him, rope still balanced around her ears. Michael let go of me and shot a hand out to Norris. "Where did you learn that?" he said, pumping his arm. Then Michael stroked Dijon's nose.

Up close, Norris looked more like a musician or an artist than a cowboy. His features were fine, his eyes a greeny blue like water, and his hands looked better suited for a piano than a rope.

"A fella in Colorado taught me," Norris said. "He called it 'reasoning.' " He slipped off his hat and wiped a sleeve across his forehead. His hair was damp and dented from the hat. "You keep them moving," he said, "give them choices. Then you let them rest when they make the right ones. It's safe for the horse and for the trainer." He put his hat back on. The brim bent down, shading his eyes, like Michael's. "God only knows how many horses I've broke like this," Norris said, "and I've only had one to buck with me."

"A rank stallion?" Michael asked.

"Na," Norris said, rubbing Dijon between the eyes, "a little filly, just as sweet as sugar — but she didn't like the saddle. Course she didn't buck till I was on her back. Had a fenceful of spectators too. That's a female for you. Takes you for a ride, then leaves your ego rolling in the dust!"

They both laughed. Pete laughed too. I didn't.

It was almost noon so I went in and fixed sandwiches and a jug of tea. I brought lunch out to the men. I wasn't hungry.

Soon, Norris and Dijon were back at work. In another hour, he had her saddled and bridled. He spent another half hour getting in and out of the saddle. Finally, he rode her. Around the ring at first, then outside the pen to where we stood. Michael stroked her head. "She's ready for a trail ride," Norris said. "We'll see y'all later." They rode off into the afternoon sun.

"That horse is as calm as an old brood mare," Michael said. "Sigmund Freud couldn't have done better." Andrew flashed through my mind.

"But Michael," I said, "don't you think she just got tired?"

"Pete says she'll be that calm tomorrow and the day after and the day after. She's learned to control her fears."

I thought about that, learning to control emotions, through sheer exhaustion. Running in circles until your lungs are aching and your mind is spinning, and nothing seems as important as rest. Maybe choices are the paths of least resistance, not really choices at all. Then just routines. That's the thing about routines that scares me so much. They're easier to live in but they numb you to the rest of life. I wondered if Dijon was better off. Easier to handle I'm sure, but better off. After that, something was missing in Dijon, spark or spirit, an aura she had the first time I saw her. Michael said whatever it was, she was better off without it.

Thinking about Michael, now, makes my throat lump up. Haven't talked to him since before Mama's funeral. I don't even know if he's still at the ranch. I could feel his restlessness coming on before I left. He kept talking about Colorado and mountains and trees. Some days I miss him so much I hurt, other days it's as though he never existed. As though last year was something I read in a book and I've never really been away from home, from Jack, from this bedroom.

I've decided to stay here until I lose the baby or until Jack wants me out, whichever comes first. Either way it's temporary. Jack thinks I'm weak because of Mama. When he realizes I'm pregnant again, he won't be so sympathetic.

To keep busy I made a list of fix-ups for the house, kind of an "inventory." God, I sound like Jack. He's kept the house decent but you can tell it hasn't been really cleaned in a year. The refrigerator's enough to give you morning sickness even if you're not pregnant. And other little things, like in the bathroom where the shower curtain came loose, Jack hung it back up with wire bread ties. Things I need to take care of before I have to go. Mama would be proud.

Mama didn't leave much of a will, just a note saying Daddy and Aunt Kate would take care of things. I've never even thought about a will. Nothing much to leave except Athene. Jack has one, of course. Wonder if he's changed it.

Donna has done most of the work, sifting through Mama's clothes, writing thank-you notes, taking care of Daddy. She amazes me. How she's changed this year. Or maybe I just don't have to help her with everything like I thought I did. Especially with Daddy. He seems to get a lot more comfort from her. Guess he blames me some for Mama. Donna says no, but I can feel it. Sometimes I see him looking at me like I'm foreign or an intrusion. God, it hurts when I see it in his eyes.

Aunt Kate hasn't been around either. Of course, she and Jack never have liked each other that much. Donna says Kate didn't have a new boyfriend all last year. It's kind of sad at the farm with no men at the house or horses in the barn. Today as I was leaving Donna's, Aunt Kate said she needs to talk with me. "Make it soon, Sarah," she said. Something in her voice set me on edge. Just my nerves, I guess. I told her I'd come tonight. Haven't been out there since the night before Mama's funeral. Don't think I can see the barn, though, without thinking of Michael. I should try to get in touch with Michael. Write a letter at least telling him about Mama.

Can't sleep. Might as well get up and do that now. Footsteps. Jack.

"Have a good nap?" he asks.

"Off and on," I say. "Is the game over?"

"No," he says, stretching out beside me. He slides his arm underneath my neck and rolls me toward him. He kisses me. Thoughts of Michael blend into Jack. Dear God, how do I keep them apart? I'll have to ask Aunt Kate. She's had enough practice.

AUNT KATE

God Almighty, I wish Vivienne had taught Donna how to cook! Don't think I can take many more of these Sunday dinners. Last week it was chicken still red at the bone. And today, roast you could patch a tire with. Bless her heart, she's trying. I shouldn't complain. I'm not doing the cooking. Of course I never claimed to be a cook. I gave up on being domestic after James said my cornbread, hurled just right, could drop a buck at forty yards. Or was it John? I always get those two confused.

Vivienne left other things undone too. Like with Sarah. She should have told her. There are secrets you take to your grave and secrets you don't. Joe knows but won't admit it. Now it falls on me.

Maybe she'll come after dark. It'll be easier. Some poet called the moon and candles "liars." But to me they just soften the truth a little, give it a glow, make even tragedy somehow beautiful. Besides, the moon means different things to different people. If it were a really bright moon, Sarah would be talking about the colors and the clouds around it and how she wished she could catch it and pull it to her heart. Donna, on the other hand, would be looking for the face of Elvis.

God, those girls are different, yet so close. I guess Vivienne and I were as close as Donna and Sarah, maybe closer. And we told each other everything. That is, she told me everything and I told her most everything. Some things even a sister couldn't forgive. Now I have to deal with Sarah. I owe it to Vivienne. I'll settle up tonight.

I feel so alone in this old house. Vivienne always said it held me longer than any man could. She was right in a way. But I'm all that's left. Me and the farm. I haven't felt this alone since Papa died. Of course, Vivienne used to say he died the same day Mama did, not on the outside but inside for sure. She was right again. Dear Jesus, I miss her.

Guess I lost her the day she married Joe. But they lived here a while and it was like we were still growing up together, taking care of each other. When Joe got them a house, Vivienne didn't want to go. I tried to convince him they'd need help with the baby coming and all, that they could save money and I could baby-sit. But Joe was too proud, damn him. Said, "Us Crawfords take care of our own."

I begged Papa to stop them. "She's only seventeen!" I cried. I was sixteen at the time and felt a lot older, but I thought age might appeal to Papa. "Only seventeen!" I cried, "Don't let Joe take her!"

Papa opened his eyes wide, wider than he had in years. He put his hands on my shoulders. "Katie," he said, "that's how old your mother was when I married her and brought her here to live with me." Then he broke down and cried. We sobbed in each other's arms, for the living and the dead.

Papa died himself in less than a year, this time on the outside too. I never felt so lonely, so deserted, like everyone I ever loved had left me. I can still see Papa laid out in the front room. I had his casket set in the corner away from the sunlight. People said things like "He looks so peaceful" and "He's with God now." He didn't look peaceful to me, just paler. As for being with God, I knew he'd rather be with Mama. I got drunk. First time in my life. Papa kept a bottle at the store. Kept it behind the counter in the center of a big ball of twine. He never drank at home but Viv and I knew about it. The night after the funeral, I went straight to the store, stuck my hand in that twine ball and pulled out a flat bottle of Jack Daniel's. It was half full and twice as much as I needed. I took it to the barn, crawled up in the hay loft, and proceeded to swallow, gag, swallow, gag, and then just swallow until I couldn't feel anything. It helped.

But the next day I felt everything — the hair follicles in my scalp, that little thing that hangs down from the back of my mouth and grates against my tongue, the space between my eyeballs. And it all hurt, one big throbbing pain. That's when I met Pat. Patrick

Martin Shields. Don't know why I remember his middle name. Maybe because he was my first, actually my second. I was at the drugstore with my head down on the counter. Doc Evatt, the druggist, was scooping ice cream. I was waiting for him to finish so I could ask him for something for my head. Pat took the stool beside me. Doc Evatt was slow, real slow, and Pat started twisting back and forth on his stool, back and forth, back and forth, driving me crazy.

"Could you stop that?" I said, not lifting my head.

"What's your problem?" he said, somewhere between defensive and sympathetic.

"My head!"

He quit twisting. "Too much Jack Daniel's?" he said.

He was kidding, but at the time I thought he was psychic.

"How can you tell?" I asked, lifting my head a little to get a look. I forgot my headache, at least temporarily, and stared into the bluest eyes I'd ever seen. His hair was reddish, more copper than red. Both hands rested on the counter. His hands looked rough but he had long, slender fingers. My mouth must have fallen open because he reached over and lifted my chin.

"I can tell by the eyes," he said, looking straight into mine. "The eyes never lie."

He swiveled back on his stool and sat there until Doc Evatt came over. He said something to Doc, then left.

"What you need, Katie?" Doc asked.

"Something for a headache," I said, staring at the door, "who was that?"

"Patrick Shields," Doc said, putting his hand to my forehead, "one heck of a carpenter. Don't think you've got a fever. Probably just one of those female headaches."

"How do you know?" I asked, still thinking about those blue eyes.

"Just guessing," Doc said taking his hand away. "Most women, you know, once a month."

I looked at Doc. "Not that!" I said, "How do you know he's a carpenter?"

"Just moved into town," Doc said, "a month or so ago. Came in here looking for work. Put a sign up by the door." Doc handed me a soda. "He's making some cabinets for the wife."

I stuck in a straw. "Whose wife?" I asked.

"My wife," Doc said, "cabinets for us."

I took a long pull on the straw. "Does he have a wife?" I tried to sound casual.

"Katie McMahan!" Doc shouted, looking over the edge of his glasses, "you're not thinking . . . He's got you by twenty years, at least."

"Oh, no," I lied. "I just have some things around the house that need fixing. You know Papa never was good with tools." I slipped off the stool. "My head's better," I said, "thanks for the soda." I headed for the door. On the way out I pulled the tack out of Patrick Shield's "Carpenter for Hire" sign, rolled the stiff paper as tight as I could, and slipped it under my shirt. It felt good.

I made contact with Pat Shields all right. After the first week, he quit charging. Just moved in and made the prettiest oak cabinets you ever saw. They're still hanging in the kitchen. So rich that when the sun hits them, they turn the whole room gold. Like right now, at sunset. I've refinished them a few times and every time I do, I get to missing Patrick Martin Shields all over again.

But it wasn't love. Just a need in me. That rush you get at first, like your heart's jumping out of your chest, and you get warm all over and dizzy just thinking about him. That's what I wanted. It blocked out everything else. But it always faded. Guess that's when real love should take over. It just didn't for me. After a while, they'd leave. I'd feel let down, so let down I'd get drunk. Then I'd go on a housecleaning binge. Vivienne said the only time I had a clean house was in between boyfriends. Pretty soon I'd discover something that needed fixing or some job I'd want done. And before I could think straight I'd end up with another boyfriend.

James, or maybe John, came after Pat. He was a roofer. Then Richard. A stone mason. I really did like him. He laid out a patio in field rock. We gathered up all these old rocks, a whole truck bed full. He set all the stones out on the grass. I can see him now. "Each one is special," he said. He'd lift each stone and hold it toward the sun like some savage, worshiping a sun-god. Then he fit them together like a mosaic that only he knew the pattern. I think about him every time I step on the patio, lifting those stones with the sun shooting off in a hundred directions.

"Oh Kate," I ask myself out loud, "why couldn't you love just one? Let just one stay and have your heart?"

"Who you talking to, Aunt Kate?" Sarah's voice comes from behind me.

"Goddamn! Sarah! You scared the shit out of me!"

"Door was open," she says, laying a hand on my shoulder. "What's got you so jumpy?"

I pat her hand, half in apology. Her fingers are long and thin. "Just a little on edge," I say. "May have been the roast beef." We both laugh. It's good to hear her laugh. It reminds me of Vivienne's laugh, years ago.

"See you haven't fixed the driveway," Sarah says, tracing bumps in the air with her hand.

"Haven't felt the need," I say. "Vivienne used to say I didn't get anything repaired unless I was horny."

"Mama never said 'horny' in her life. She didn't even know the meaning of the word."

"What she said was unless I needed a man. But don't be so sure what she knew and didn't know." I open the refrigerator. "Get you a beer?"

"Maybe one," Sarah says.

"Take it into the front room," I say. I watch her walk. She looks so much like Vivienne did at her age, not her features but the way the light plays off her face, the way she moves. Sarah sits on the sofa. I sit beside her and feel awkward as hell. I think about Papa laid out in the corner. Wonder if he's with Mama. Sarah's watching me, waiting. I'm not ready so I say, "See that mantel-piece? It was made the same year you were born."

"Pretty old, huh?" she says, smiling.

"No, not to me. It doesn't seem all that long ago. It's made of walnut."

"What?" Sarah says.

"The mantel," I say. I get up and run my hand across it. Dust particles twist in the air. "Walnut," I say rubbing my hands together, "hand-hewn."

Sarah takes a sip of her beer. "Who made it?" she asks.

"A carpenter. He was living with me here when you were born. Still pretty, isn't it? He said this walnut should last forever."

Sarah nods. She takes a deeper pull on the beer. "No offense, Aunt Kate, but reckon how many boyfriends you've had?"

"If I think really hard," I say, counting on my fingers, "I could tell you. I'd have to go from room to room, though, to make sure."

"How do you keep them apart?"

"They all made something or fixed something or left something in the house," I say, "all craftsmen — artists in a way." Sarah looks serious, too serious. I try to lighten her up. "You're not trying to break my record, are you?"

She smiles. "Not hardly, Aunt Kate. For me, two is one too many." Then she stares into space as though she might cry. Too soon, I think.

"But damn, Sarah," I say, slapping her on the leg, "a veterinarian! Why didn't I think of that? I never got beyond the house!" She's back with me. We drink together.

"One time while you were gone," I say, "when I was feeling especially mean, I told old Joe, looks like he'd be proud to have a 'doctor' in the family. Really pissed him off. But what pissed him off even worse was when Donna spoke right up and said, 'We do have a doctor in the family — Andrew Webster, Ph.D.' Joe said, 'doctor, like hell,' and retreated to his garden."

I'm laughing by now and I get Sarah started. We both laugh till we hurt, just like I've seen her and Donna do hundreds of times, just like Viv and I used to do. A laugh between sisters.

I go for another beer. When I come back, Sarah's standing by the mantelpiece, rubbing it as though she's appreciating it for the first time. "Aunt Kate," she says, "didn't you love any of them?"

"I love the house," I say, popping the fresh can. "They're all a part, so in that way, I love them. But, by then my heart was already gone."

"To the mantelpiece man?" Sarah asks.

My hands shakes. A little stream of beer rolls down my arm. "Before that," I say. I'm as ready now as I'll ever be, I think. "Sit down, Sarah." I take her arm and guide her back to the sofa, "That's what I want to talk to you about."

"Your first love?" she says, staring into my eyes.

"That and Vivienne's first love."

"Mama's?" Sarah asks. She takes a long pull on her beer. The last of the can, I know, by the grimace on her face.

"Viv and I depended on each other. We had to. After Mama died early and Papa stayed so busy at the store. We had the farm but Papa did better in selling. He loved that store, its shelves and rows and bins. And he had everything — string, fireball jawbreakers, nails, sweet feed, cloth, pencils, Blue-Horse paper. You ever had a fireball, Sarah?"

She shakes her head. "Then you don't know what you're missing. They're hot as hell, turn your tongue red then white, and make your stomach ache. We loved them. Kind of like smoking for a

kid. God, I need a cigarette. You mind?'' Sarah shakes her head.
I know she's lying but I light one anyway. I suck in hard. The
smoke feels good, so good I don't want to breathe out. But I have
to. I take a second drag.

"Papa had everything all bottled or stacked, organized and
counted. He said nature couldn't mess up his store like it could
crops and people. So he stayed in the store more and more after
Mama died.'' I finish off my second beer. "This stuff goes straight
through you,'' I say, "be back in a minute.''

When I come back, Sarah's holding two fresh cans. She hands
me one and pops the other one for herself.

"But, see, we still had the farm to think about.'' I open my can
and take a swallow. "So Papa rented out parcels of land and hired
on tenant farmers to take care of things out here. Vivienne and I
managed the house on our own. She cooked, I cleaned, we both
did school work and we both read a lot. Mostly classics back then.
Our mother had quite a collection — Shakespeare's plays, the *Illiad*
and the *Odyssey*, Dickens' novels, a pioneer book or two by James
Fenimore Cooper — mostly fiction. Of course, at that age you
read everything like it's God's truth. And we stayed out of trouble
until . . . '' I look over at Papa's corner and wonder if he's listening.

"Until?'' Sarah says. She's on the edge of the sofa, breathing
in my smoke.

I shift the ashtray, "Until the summer Samuel Harrison and his
family came to live at the farm. I was sixteen at the time, Viv was
seventeen. Samuel Harrison had a son, named David, the same age
as Vivienne. And a daughter, Opal, about four, I think.'' I wipe
the sweat from the can and take a pull. "He told Papa that his first
wife died in childbirth. You can just bet that got to Papa. And
Samuel said his second wife went back home to her parents after
Opal was born. Papa said a man like that would work hard to keep
his mind off his sadness. Papa was right. He just didn't realize what
Samuel Harrison would work hard at.'' I light another cigarette and
blow the smoke away from Sarah, toward Papa's corner. Sarah
doesn't seem to notice. She's staring into my eyes.

I take another long drag then continue, "Viv and I hung around
the Harrison household at first to play with Opal. We pretended
she was our little sister, made a big fuss over her. She had sky-
blue eyes and the reddest hair I've ever seen. Vivienne made Opal
a dress, buttercup yellow, and embroidered little daisies all over

the collar. We'd put Opal on Tar Baby, that was our pony's name, and lead her around the barn like a princess. Had her looking like Shirley Temple. I used to think about little Opal everytime Viv got Donna all dolled up for those recitals. Remember how Donna looked? Remember that poodle costume?''

Sarah nods. "Go on about Opal," she says.

"Opal wasn't the problem. What happened is your mother started spending more time with David than she did Opal. David looked like his father, only younger of course, handsome and just busting out of his jeans, like he was outgrowing everything he put on. Only his hands didn't go with the rest of him. They were artist hands, long fingers, smooth nails, knuckles not yet knotted with work. A little young for my taste, but not Vivienne's." Sarah's eyes widen. She takes a long drink.

"David told her about places he'd worked. Pennsylvania with its big red barns, Georgia with black dirt and tobacco farms, Kentucky's blue grass that wasn't really blue. Viv hung on his every word. Every night she'd repeat them to me. David said he hoped his family would go out West, get their own place and raise whatever they raise out there. Just so it was theirs and nobody else's.

"Vivienne and David fell for each other faster than star-crossed lovers. She was so pretty and hungry for the world. He was handsome and had seen a good part of it, even if it was from tenant shacks. I'm sure Papa and even Samuel Harrison would have put an end to it, early on, if they had known then. But Papa was busy with the store and Samuel was busy with me."

Sarah reached for a cigarette, touched her belly with her other hand, then slipped the cigarette back in the pack.

"I can still see Samuel Harrison. God, Sarah, he was handsome, so masculine. Eyes greener than summer grass. Moustache thickest at the corners of his mouth. Dark hair curling around his ears. Arms shiny brown from the sun." I still get a rush just thinking about him.

Sarah touches me on the knee. "Go on," she says.

"I always wondered why he went for me instead of your mother. She was prettier. Maybe pretty didn't matter and I just looked more willing. Hell! I was for him." I stop to pull on my beer. It's empty. Sarah goes for another one. I can still feel Samuel Harrison, tall and dark, pulling me up the ladder into the hayloft. Straw pricking my neck as he kissed me up one side and down the other. Whispering love words the whole time.

Sarah hands me the beer. It's already popped. "Go on," she says again.

"It was good, too Goddamn good for a sixteen-year-old farm girl." I take a drink. It's cold all the way down. "Because, Sarah, it never was that way again. Memories of him haunted me, came between me and every other lover I had, like a fog rolling in so thick I couldn't even see the face in front of me."

"Tell me about Mama," Sarah says. Her voice sounds tight, urgent.

"While I was in the hayloft making love with Samuel Harrison, Vivienne and David were in the back room of the tenant house doing the same." Sarah reaches for a cigarette again. This time she doesn't put it back. "Samuel caught them. They left the next day." Sarah's trying to light up but her hand is shaking too hard. I think about stopping here, letting her calm down, but I want to get this done. I light the cigarette for her. She inhales. "I don't think they would have left," I say, watching her closely, "if they'd known about Vivienne." Sarah exhales, then gulps for air like she's drowning. "You okay?" I ask her.

She nods. "Go on," Sarah whispers. That same look she used to get as a teenager. When she got upset at home, she'd come over to the farm and crawl up in the barn loft. I'd leave her alone to cry or scream or cuss or whatever made her feel better. Then she'd come looking for me and I'd hand her a cigarette. Sometimes she wouldn't even tell me what was wrong. We'd just sit together smoking and talking about a beautiful sunset or horseback-riding or a good book until she was ready to go home.

"But," I say, "at any rate the Harrisons did leave. And there was Joe Crawford who'd been hanging around Vivienne since grade school. They got married fast with Joe still amazed at his good fortune." Sarah stares into space. Her cigarette rolls off her fingertips. I retrieve it, grind it in the ash tray, then take both my hands and turn her face toward me. "When you came along, Joe made a big to-do over being a father. At the time I thought he must have a room-temperature IQ. Now I realize he knew. But he never let on." I let go. Sarah's face collapses into her own hands. I put my arms around her shoulders, hold her close and just let her cry.

The phone rings. I leave Sarah to answer. "It's Jack," I say. Sarah shakes her head. "She can't come to the phone. No, Jack, she's fine. She's in the bathroom." I roll my eyes at Sarah. "Afterwhile. Just ice tea. Okay, Jack, I promise." I hang up. Poor Jack,

I think to myself, he lives in a world of balance and absolutes. I don't think he knows there's a whole other world. Shadows, longings, passions he doesn't feel, at least I don't think so. But Sarah does. I can see it in those Harrison eyes.

She's quit crying. "Jack wanted to know if you're feeling all right. I said you were. Are you?"

She nods.

"Want to stay here? You know you don't have to go back to Jack."

Sarah smiles and pats me on the arm. "I'll go home, at least for the night. I need to lie down."

I walk her to the car. The moon is full or almost, I can't tell the difference when it's this bright. We both cast long shadows.

Sarah turns to me. The moon illuminates her face. "Did you ever hear from them, Aunt Kate, either one?"

I lift my arm out from my body, watch its shadow streak across the driveway. "No," I say, "and I never told Vivienne about me and Samuel. I figured their leaving had as much to do with me as it did her. She might not have forgiven me." I look for forgiveness in Sarah's eyes but they are somewhere else.

"I didn't come out unscathed. I used up my womanhood loving and hating Samuel for what he'd done to me in that musty hayloft. Now, I realize he was just a big horny farmer, scraping for a living, and desperately missing his wives. But for me, he became a Romantic hero, not the Harlequin kind, but the noble savage of Byron and Shelley and Coleridge's poetry. I'll bet that's what your veterinarian is to you, some kind of hero."

"Maybe so," she says. She opens the car door. Her shadow folds, collapses.

"Still," I say, more to myself than to Sarah, "if I could trade hindsight for illusion, I don't think I would. What a tedious life it would have been, married to some mechanic or teacher or mortician, going to choir practice on Wednesday, playing bingo on Friday."

"Maybe so," Sarah says again, but her mind is somewhere else. She cranks the engine. I watch her drive away.

"Rest in peace, Vivienne!" I shout to the moon. I won't and Sarah has a long way to go.

PART IV

BIRTH

ANDREW

Donna looks upset.

"I got here as soon as I could," I tell her. She glares at me, then back across the waiting room at Jack.

"Is Sarah all right?" I ask.

"SHE is," Donna says in a loud whisper, "but that sorry husband of hers." She flips her hand in his direction like she's trying to shake off something nasty. "He called me 'Prima Donna Dingbat.'"

"What on earth for?" I say, thinking of several possibilites.

"Because I didn't call him."

"You didn't?"

Donna looks me in the face, her eyes full of sincerity. "I was at Sarah's when she went into labor, so I drove over here just as fast as I could and got her admitted. He SHOULD be grateful." She catches her breath. "And I would have called him, but after I called you and Aunt Kate and Daddy and Holly's Hair and Then Some — I had to cancel my appointment — I ran out of quarters."

I look at Jack. He seems oblivious to everything around him. You'd think Sarah were dying instead of giving birth. In the opposite corner is Joe. Buddha-like, belly and all, staring at the television. It isn't turned on. Kate's got the other corner. Smoking a cigarette and nursing a cup of coffee as if she's spiked it. She probably has.

After sixteen years of living with these people, I thought nothing they could say or do would surprise me. When I married Donna, my family and friends kidded me about getting used to mushy food, i-n-g without the g, "S-u-u-u-r" and "May-yam." But it's not the way they eat or even talk, although they do have a knack for backyard metaphors, that's so peculiar about them. It's the way they think and, as a result, act that makes you wonder about oxygen deprivation south of the Mason-Dixon.

Take Mr. Crawford's white pickle. It's suspended in a bottle of vinegar, sitting on the living room mantel. "A conversation piece," he calls it. It looks like a giant's thumb or huge growth or a man's vital organ floating around in vinegar. Guests invariably ask what it is. Old Joe says "a cucumber." Just that and no more until someone asks how he got it through the small mouth of the bottle without cutting it or why it's not green. That's what he waits for, lives for, someone asking about the mystery of his huge albino cucumber.

He won't tell me. Each time I ask, he just sits there, sphinx-like, letting me guess and guess, while he clicks his teeth or laughs at my hypotheses or says, "Do ya give up?" I refuse. I'll figure out that damn pickle as soon as I don't have so many other matters on my mind. My tenure project, for one.

It's that sort of behavior you have to get used to. And I thought I had until Sarah came home. I could understand her returning to see about her mother and, of course, staying for the funeral. But afterward, she just moved back in with Jack as though she hadn't been away for the past year. And Jack let her. Amazing. They were back at Sunday dinner like they'd never missed a pot roast. A regular couple just sitting there in domestic bliss, passing the rice and green beans.

Of course, I relieved the tension by keeping the dinner conversation going. I'd told interesting tidbits I'd read in *Time* or the latest *Journal of the American Medical Association*; we in the business call it JAMA. But if Sarah were my wife, absconding with another man, I'd never let her back in my house. Not that Donna would even consider leaving me for another man or for any reason that I can think of.

I told Donna I would offer them counseling but she said it might start something. She's probably right. If I counseled every troubled marriage I've seen, I'd never get my project done. The whole family treats Sarah as though she's never been away, except Joe, who's been extremely withdrawn from all of us since Vivienne's death.

Then Sarah turns up pregnant. We didn't even know it until two months ago. My Donna popped out the second month, but she was carrying twins. When Donna told me Sarah's due date, I figured backwards. Nine months, to the day, when Vivienne was buried.

"Sarah's cutting it close," I told Donna. But Donna said that was Jack's calculations, not Sarah's.

I stare across the waiting room. It hits me. I think out loud, "Sarah's not due for two more months, is she?"

Jack jumps to attention, "one month and twenty-eight days," he says, panic evident in his voice. "She made it to six months one time — that was the longest." He wrings his hands. "But seven months and two days. That's better. Much better for both of them." He's talking more to himself than to us.

I look at Donna. She rolls her eyes and whispers, "Sarah saw her doctor this morning. He said she was ready."

"Tell Jack," I whisper back. "Maybe that will help calm his nerves."

"Mama died seven months ago, Andrew, just seven," she says. "Better he worry about premature than other things." She lifts her eyebrows to punctuate "other things."

I don't know why we're debating due dates. For God's sake, the man's had a vasectomy! I'm not supposed to know, but Sarah told Donna and, of course, Donna told me.

"Think I'll turn on the TV," Donna says, reaching for the dial, "Oprah's supposed to be about UFOs today." She begins flipping through stations.

"Wait," Joe says, leaning forward, breaking his Buddha pose. "Turn back."

"What, Daddy?"

"Turn back."

"To what?" Donna says, turning the dial slowly.

"The black and white one. I don't know the number," he says. "Stop! That's it." He shifts in his chair, "Mayberry RFD, you know, Andy Griffin."

I say, "It's Andy Griff-ith."

"That's what I said, Andy Griffin. Leave it there, Donna."

"I want to see 'Oprah,' " Donna says, disappointment obvious in her voice. "It's about UFOs, Daddy. Some people who've been kidnapped by aliens."

Jack looks up. "Kidnapped?" he says, his voice almost high.

"Just television," I say. "Good God, he's on edge," I whisper to Donna. She doesn't hear me.

"They've all been examined by aliens," Donna is saying, "touched inside and out."

"That's a bunch of bull," Joe says, not taking his eyes off Andy Griffith. "They just say that to get on TV."

"Anybody need coffee?" Kate says, disappearing through the door before I can answer.

"How long has it been?" I ask.

"What?" Donna says.

"How long has Sarah been in labor?"

"Two hours," Donna says.

Jack looks at his watch. "Two hours, fourteen minutes," he says.

"You've got a long time yet," Donna says. "I was in labor twelve hours, ten of those hard labor and I do mean hard. Wasn't I, Andrew?"

"Yes," I say, not really wanting to remember.

"And Andrew was with me the whole time, holding my hand, rubbing my forehead. Weren't you, honey?" She smiles at me sweetly.

"Yes," I say, "the whole time." The delivery room comes floating back to me like a bad dream. Donna yelling, voices saying "push, Mrs. Webster, push." The stirrups and those umbilical cords, all wet and coiled. I swallow hard and stare at Don Knotts.

"This is the one," Joe says, "where a counterfeiter comes to Mayberry and pretends to be a barber." He starts laughing. "Course he can't cut hair worth a hoot and Andy gets suspicious."

I'm starting to feel claustrophobic. "Think I'll go out for a stretch," I tell Donna.

"Maybe you'd better pick us up a bucket of chicken while you're out," Donna says. "It's right across the highway." She looks at Joe and Jack. "Does that suit y'all?" Neither answers. "Make it extra crispy," she calls after me.

I detour the labor room, take the stairs, push through the glass double doors and into the wide-open day. A pretty day. Slight chill to the air but almost spring-like. The buds on the red maples are ready to burst open. At home it would be the sugar maples, but not for another month at least.

Donna thinks it's bitter cold, but she doesn't know what cold is. At home there's probably snow on the ground, maybe even into April. I'll bet the kids are skating as I did as a child. Every winter when the city would send in snow plows to clear the streets, they'd push up berms of snow in the school yard. Then they'd release water from the fire hydrant to make layers of ice within the berm. Mother wouldn't let me skate on ponds, but I could skate all winter in the school yard. Dad would come for me every evening after work. It would be almost dark by then. I would carry my skates over my shoulder and we'd walk home, like a Currier and Ives Christmas card.

When summer came, sometimes we'd drive up to Berkshire Hills. Dad and I would hike while Mother and Grandmother and Aunt Ruth would go to concerts at Tanglewood Music Shed. Other summers we'd head east to Cape Cod. Those beaches are different from these down here. Shorter stretches of sand framed between rock, more private than the miles and miles of Southern beaches. You could buy French rolls stuffed with lobster right on the shore.

That was when Dad was alive. All that stopped the year he died. I was ten, but never a child again. Grandmother moved in with us. Then Aunt Ruth. They called me "the little man of the house." All three took it upon themselves to make Andrew Junior into the perfect Andrew Senior. Grandmother was as proper as a finger bowl. She appointed herself etiquette warden. "You can," she would say, "but you may not." Aunt Ruth became the education warden. She was a teacher and wanted me to benefit from her vast knowledge. Actually, I did learn a wealth of her trivia, but better, I learned to collect my own, a trait that has become useful in adulthood.

For Mother I became her only reason for living, "all I have left." She was a walking record of what "your father did" and didn't do, "your father would like" and wouldn't like.

I don't go home very often. For one reason, Donna doesn't like to fly. I went for Grandmother's funeral by myself. It reminded me so much of Dad's death that I didn't sleep for days. I've only been a few times since then. If Mother and Aunt Ruth know I'm coming, they save up every broken appliance, tax notice, and household repair job for me. Last time I went home, the first thing

Mother said was, "Oh, Andrew, you're getting a bald spot just like your father. Come see, Ruth."

"Tut, tut, tut," Aunt Ruth's voice came from somewhere behind me, "he certainly is, just like Andrew Sr."

Then both of them in unison said, "So good to have a man in the house." And out came a list of "things for Andrew to do." I haven't been back.

Maybe I'll take the twins after school is out. I'd like for them to see places I loved as a child. I'll get Mother to fix mutton and mint jelly for them. I can hear what Donna will say, "Oh, Andrew, I just can't eat a little lamb!"

"But they can sure chow down on little chicks," I say out loud as I reach Kentucky Fried Chicken.

"Pardon me, sir?" the cashier says.

"Barrel of chicken," I say. "Make it extra crispy."

"Fresh air helped," I tell Donna, handing her the barrel.

She distributes the chicken. "Drumsticks for Daddy. White meat for Aunt Kate. Jack, what do you want?"

"What?"

"What piece do you want?"

He shakes his head. "Not hungry."

Donna fishes out a roll, and sets it on a napkin beside his chair. "You need your strength," she says, "for Sarah." I can hear Vivienne in her voice.

I pass on the chicken too. The "Andy Griffith Show" is going off. Joe whistles along. Donna commandeers the dial for the last half of "Oprah."

"You were really kidnapped?" Oprah is saying.

"Yes," says a rather plain woman, probably in her mid-thirties.

Oprah glances out to the audience, then back to the guest, "What exactly did they do to you?"

"They took off my clothes," the woman says, her eyes down, "and examined me. Then they erased my memory."

A man, one of the few in the audience, stands up. Oprah points the microphone in his face. "If they erased your memory," he says, looking around for support, "how do you know they they took off your clothes and examined you?"

"I dream about it," she says, "every night. I see what they're doing to me in my dreams." The audience snickers.

Kate puts down her coffee. "Isn't there a term, Andrew," she asks, "for those kinds of dreams?"

"Yes," I say, "and it has nothing to do with aliens. It's a subconscious manifestation of sexual frustration."

Donna picks at the crust on her chicken. "Maybe that's just what the aliens want you experts to think." She says "experts" as if it's doubtful.

"Sounds like stuff for a research project to me," Kate says. "Alien-Induced Sex Dreams: Myth or Reality?"

"Tell them about your real project," Donna says, folding a napkin into smaller and smaller squares. "He's been working on it for-e-v-e-r."

I clear my throat. Joe gets up and switches channels. Jack stares at the roll beside him. Kate picks up a magazine, looks up and says, "Go ahead, I'm listening."

I clear my throat again. "My research project," I say, "is the effect of early adolescence on female fraternal twins. It's like analyzing why you and Vivienne turned out so differently. Or why Donna and Sarah are so different." I have all of their attention now. "The age difference and birth order are automatically eliminated as factors with twins, yet with fraternal twins the genes are as different as . . ."

Voices from the hallway interrupt me. "It's over here, Mama. I smell chicken. Do you?" Two women enter the waiting room. Both are the same shade of blond and both are wearing sweat suits, the same size, I'd guess, but the fit is significantly different. The younger woman, about Donna's age I think, is wearing pink, hot pink. The other woman is an older version of the first. She's wearing purple, stretched to the limit, particularly in the waist.

I look at Donna. She throws her second piece of chicken back into the bucket and sucks in her stomach.

The one in purple says, "Look at all these people. Must be a full moon. That's when babies like to come."

"Hello," Donna says, as though she's the waiting room hostess.

"Hey," the younger one says. "You waiting for a grandbaby?"

Donna's eyes bulge. "Lord, no!" she says, "My sister's having a baby."

"My daughter is," the younger one says, "her first."

The purple woman speaks up, "She ain't but eighteen."

"Mama, quit worrying. Tina'll do just fine," the pink one says, pointing her mother toward chairs near Jack. Then to Donna, "I weren't but seventeen when I had Tina." Joe catches her last words and looks in her direction.

The pink one looks at me. "Whose baby you waiting on?" she asks.

"He's with me," Donna says.

"You here for a baby that ain't even yours?"

"That's correct," I say, thinking to myself, she has a point.

The two women sit between Kate and Jack. The younger one points at Joe and says to Donna, "Who's he waiting on?"

"My sister's baby," Donna says. "He's our daddy."

"And her?" She points to Kate. I expect Kate to say something nasty but she doesn't.

"Aunt," Donna says. "My mother's dead," she adds, like she's enjoying "20 questions."

Suddenly Jack jumps up, looks at his watch, crams his hands in his pockets, then sits back down. "He must be the father," the pink one says.

Donna nods.

The woman in purple speaks up again. "At least they know who the father is!"

"Y'all want some chicken," Donna says offering the bucket. "We had some left."

"Thanks," the pink one says, then to her mother, "Tina knows. And so do we. She ain't been with but no one but Brian. She just don't want to marry him."

"It ain't what she *wants* to do, Mary Beth," the purple one says, "it's what she *should* do." She reaches in the bucket and pulls out a thigh.

"I married Marvin," the pink Mary Beth says. She bites into a drumstick. "And look what it got me." She turns to Donna. "Got any napkins?" She chews a few times. "Spent every penny we had on that stock car, replacing this, adding on that. Never won a race

110]

in his life. Not that paid anyway." She finally swallows. "I raised her by myself and she turned out just fine."

"I helped raise Tina, too. Alls I'm saying is a baby needs a father." She looks to us for support. We all nod, even Joe.

Then both blonds sit there eating MY chicken, but in silence. Just as I'm thinking "Thank God, for the quiet," Mary Beth starts to coughing. "Dear Jesus!" I shout, "She's choking on a chicken bone!"

As I jerk her up and commence the Heimlich Maneuver, she starts sputtering, "My little Tina's just a baby herself!" I let go. She collapses into her mother's arms. "My baby's having a baby," she cries. "Seems like just yesterday she was playing with Nadine!" Her mother holds her close and rocks her as best she can on the upholstered seat. The vinyl squeaks back and forth.

The purple Mama looks at Donna. "Nadine's her cabbage patch doll. I give it to her when she was seven." Donna's eyes fill with tears. She starts to sniffle.

"Donna," I whisper, "what's wrong with you?"

"That could be our little Scarlet or Charlotte in just a few years," she says. The thought is alarming. My chest feels tight. More babies. More women all around.

"Maybe it'll be a boy," the purple Mama says.

Joe turns around. "Sarah?" he says, "a boy?"

"No, Daddy," Donna says, "Tina." He turns back to the television.

"Tina was carrying low," the purple Mama says, "low and out."

Mary Beth quits crying, "I carried her high and around." She holds out her sweat shirt to demonstrate. Jack watches in rapt attention. He holds his hands out and shapes a pregnant abdomen in front of himself.

"I carried low and out and high and around," Donna says, caught up in their pregnancy trivia. They look at Donna. "Twins," she says, smiling proudly.

"Twins!" shouts Mary Beth. She's crying again. No one else seems bothered. Joe has finished "Perry Mason" and is engrossed in an old episode of "Cannon." Kate's still drinking out of her coffee cup but the coffee is long gone.

I'll go stark raving mad if I don't get out of here, I think to myself. I start to stand up when an adolescent boy bursts through the doorway. He's wearing a block C jacket studded with various balls and bars. "What have you done to her?" he shouts.

"You idiot!" Mary Beth shouts back. "It's what you done to her! Now she's in the labor room." Then to her mother, "My baby's in labor!" Her crying reaches new intensity.

"Where's it at?" he demands, looking around the room as if there may be a secret passage.

"Brian, you can't go in there," says the purple Mama. "She don't want nobody with her."

"It's my baby!" he shouts, his voice cracking. "She needs me!"

Kate sets down her cup. She refills it from a bottle in her purse. "Down the hall to the right," she says. He disappears through the doorway. Kate lifts her cup and toasts the air. "To a spunky kid," she says. "Goddamn spunky kid."

JACK

How long can this labor thing go on? It never took this long to miscarry. Maybe it's a good sign. Or maybe not. They had me sign a release in case of surgery. They may not tell me right away if they have to operate. What if she needs blood? She's A-positive. I could be out getting donors right now down at the car lot. If I could just do something. I feel so damn useless in here.

Sarah never told me she was pregnant, never came right out and said, "Jack, I'm going to have a baby." She didn't put old sheets on the bed or try to stop our lovemaking. But I got suspicious early on. After you've been through it as many times as I have, you know. Things start to feel different.

Still, I didn't say anything about it until the kicking started. One night we were settled in bed, me outlining Sarah's back with my chest, my hand across her abdomen, when I felt a bump. I felt it again right against my wrist. I thought it was my pulse at first, then it bumped again, this time in my palm.

"Sarah!" I shouted, "Wake up! Did you feel that?" But she was already awake.

"A week," she said, not looking at me, "it's been kicking a week." Out of all the others we lost, she'd only felt one of them kick. I never felt it though. This was my first. I couldn't get it off my mind. It was like those hot-cold chills I used to get in high school right before a game, still get the morning of a big sale.

We didn't talk much about it for a while. Sarah seemed hesitant and I didn't want to jinx anything. Her obstetrician, Dr. Fleming, suggested tests because of her age and to see how far along she was. She wouldn't let him. I think she was right. I looked it up in a medical book, and there's a slight chance, about one in 250, the tests could cause a miscarriage. With her history, we agreed, even that was too high.

I looked up something else too. The chances of conceiving after a vasectomy. Less than one on one hundred and that's if the operation is botched. Not very good odds. But still possible. I've learned one thing in the past year — nothing's absolute.

But, Dear God, I don't see why she won't let me be with her right now. She says she doesn't want me to see her like that, but she needs me. I need to be there.

Things can go wrong. Last time she miscarried, the doctor said she could bleed to death if she had another one. Sarah and I didn't talk about that either, but it's been on my mind right along with feeling that baby move. She doesn't realize how badly a baby needs its mother. I do. And so does Tommy.

When I told him Sarah was pregnant again, Tommy said, "Be there for her no matter what." Then he put both hands on my shoulders and said, "But remember, she's a lot like your mama."

How can I be there for her, damn it, if she won't let me in the labor room?

I first met Sarah in, of all things, a poetry class. God only knows why I took it. My advisor said it'd do me good to get away from figures. He meant numbers, but there was Sarah with a figure I couldn't stay away from. It wasn't just her body that attracted me. She would talk with such passion about poems that didn't mean a thing to me the first time I read them. But after I heard her, I'd go back, reread them, and see what she meant. About the only one I remember now, though, is "Do Not Go Gentle" by Dylan somebody. It was about a son talking to his dying father, telling him not to give in to what life was dealing him, to fight back. I read it to Tommy. "I like it, Jack," he said, "good advice for living fathers as well as dying ones."

All semester while most of us struggled for meaning, Sarah and a few other artsy types seemed to live the lines. That was what I loved about her. Her knack for riding passion like a wild horse to some unknown destination. I wanted to be there to watch her ride and to catch her if she fell. When I was feeling especially poetical I told that to Tommy, hoping he wouldn't laugh. He didn't. He just said, "Poetry class may be rubbing off on you, Jack, but make sure Sarah's fall doesn't bring you down too." Then he said something else I thought about over and over last year when Sarah left. "She's hungry," he said, his voice shaking, "just like your mama was."

There sits Donna Jean chatting like her sister's having a tooth filled instead of maybe bleeding to death. Damn hair brain. I could choke her. If I hadn't come home for lunch and found Sarah missing, no telling when Donna would have called. I was afraid Sarah had left again. Thank God, I called Dr. Fleming's office and found out.

No quarter! Not even Donna Jean can be that stupid. Maybe Sarah told her not to call me. No, Sarah wouldn't do that, not my Sarah. Who the hell am I kidding? She's not my Sarah anymore and no telling what she'd do!

She hadn't been home a month when she got on this job kick. One morning out of the blue she said, "Jack, I need a job."

"You're not well enough," I say.

"I need a job," she repeated, stabbing her grapefruit.

"Why?" I asked.

She laid down her spoon. "Because I need the money."

"Your name's still on the checking account."

"I know."

"Well?"

"I need my own money." She said "own" like the word was sacred.

"Doing what?" I asked, playing along.

"Office work." A note of excitement in her voice.

"I could probably find you a spot in the salesroom," I said, warming to the idea, "or the service department."

She shook her head. Her hair stood out like it was charged. Then she got up and left the table like I'd insulted her, offering her my money and a job in my business. Damn! She's hard to understand. After the baby started kicking, she gave up on the job idea. I convinced her it might be too much of a strain. So she goes on this housecleaning binge. Starting with our closet. She threw out arm loads of my old stuff. Then she went out and bought me something new for everything she got rid of. Especially underwear. She bought me a huge stack of Hanes. I swear, I think I could go a whole year without having to wash a single pair. She sewed back on buttons I didn't even realize had come off. And she had all my loafers reheeled.

Cid, down at the lot, said it was "nesting instinct." He said when his wife was pregnant she bought a set of World Books, and zebra-striped bed sheets, and Franklin Mint miniature Russian music boxes. Then she bought a jogging outfit for every day of the week. To get back in shape, she said, after the baby came. Cid said she never could get into the little shorts.

Steve said his wife was the same way only with leotards, all colors, to do yoga, meditate, be calm around the baby. Didn't work, he said, she cut an outfit into tiny little pieces every time the baby had a bad night. Even the tights. Left little stretchy shreds all in the carpet.

But Sarah did the opposite. She gave away all her dresses except a few loose ones. Kept a denim skirt, a few pairs of jeans, some shirts and sweaters. That's about it except for some moccasin-like shoes and a pair of sandals. I know because I checked her side of the closet. First time ever my side was fuller than hers. When I asked why most of her stuff was gone she said it was old or didn't fit or out of style.

Just kidding, one day I said, "Sarah, did you clean out your jewelry box, too?"

[115

She was fixing sandwiches. She got a funny look on her face and didn't say anything right away. "Why do you ask?" She stared at the bread.

"I was just kidding," I said, "but did you?"

"Just a few things to Donna's girls," she said, tossing some chips on my plate. "That's all."

That night while she was taking a shower I looked in her jewelry box. Practically empty except her wedding band, some gold earrings I gave her for our tenth anniversary, an opal ring of her mother's, some silver loops, and a turquoise bracelet I didn't recognize. That was it!

I wasn't positive what should have been in there but I knew the important pieces that were missing, ones I'd given her. A Kruggerand necklace, a string of pearls — real pearls — and a sapphire and diamond ring. I don't know if she sold them or gave them away or lost them or what the hell she did with them. Maybe she really was desperate for her "own" money. Hell! That damn Krugerrand was probably worth $400 at least. I could check the market to find out exactly. God, I hope she didn't give it away!

Another day when I came home for lunch, Sarah was balanced up on a chair in front of the bookshelf, raining down books into two loose piles. "What are you doing?" I asked.

"Guess," she said, her back to me.

"Cleaning out the bookshelf."

"Bingo!"

"All of the books?"

"Most," she said. "I've already read them and you're not going to. There aren't any *Consumer Guides* up here."

"So what are you going to do with them? Throw them away?" I knew that'd get her.

"Of course not," she said, an edge to her voice. "I'm giving them to Scarlet and Charlotte." She stopped dropping books and turned around. "One pile's classics. The other's modern."

"Who gets what?" I asked. "Let me guess. Charlotte gets the classics and Scarlet gets the fun stuff."

"That's what I had in mind." She stared across the room at the fireplace. It held a small flame. "But maybe I should do it the other way around. It might help both of them. What do you think?"

"I think Scarlet would be bored silly. Who knows about Charlotte."

"Maybe I'll just mix them up," she said, straining for the upper shelf.

"Let me get them," I said, pulling her off the chair and cleared the top shelf with one hand. Dust shot out and drifted down on both of us.

"I could have done it myself," Sarah said, faking a cough. Dust balls settled in the outer curves of her hair. I picked out several clumps. Her hair felt soft.

"Better dust fall, than you, sweetheart," I said in a Bogart voice that surprised even me. We both laughed and I held her close. The baby moved, our baby.

OUR baby! Who the hell am I kidding? How would I know it's mine? But it might be. Sarah hasn't been in contact with that horse jerk since she's come home to me. Not that I know of. Hasn't called him anyway. I check the phone bill every month. I pick up the mail on the way home to lunch every day too. No suspicious letters. Not that I'm spying on her. He's probably moved on to greener pastures by now — some other man's wife and horse.

I've got to quit thinking like this. Sarah's my wife. She would have gone back if the baby wasn't mine. At least, I think she would.

What's Andrew staring at? He seems quieter than usual. No medi-facts, thank God. I couldn't take any today.

There sits Joe. I don't know why he's here. He's never treated Sarah right. Not that he's been mean or anything, just never acted warm toward her or proud of her like he's been with Donna Jean. Not as long as I've known them. Truth is, at times I've thought he'd rather have me in the family than Sarah.

And Kate. If she had her way, she'd probably be in there with Sarah getting her drunk out of her mind — "to ease the pain." I bet she'll try to get in touch with that vet just as soon as this is over. That's where Sarah met him in the first place — at Kate's farm. Kate probably set it up.

God! I'm getting paranoid. I've got to calm down. Maybe I'll call Tommy. A good father, unlike Joe. The best. A doffer at the Stevens Mill and proud of it. Says he'll doff to the day he dies.

But Tommy always wanted more for me — "brainwork" he called it. Tommy and I didn't have time for many father-son things but he saw to it I did well in school. That's the only way he'd let me play basketball. And he sent me to college. Almost every day

[117

when he got home from work, he'd ask questions that he or another doffer had thought of — Who has the best deal on Chevys in town? How much money does a bank president make? How many types of poisonous snakes are there in the South? I'd have to come up with an answer or he'd say "What am I paying for?" or "You should know, Mr. College." So if I didn't know the answer, I'd look it up in an encyclopedia or almanac or fact book or call somebody who did know. It was good training. Not for boring people to death, like Andrew, but for business.

Andrew's disappeared. Maybe he's gone home. Not Donna Jean. Still reading a magazine. Quiet for a change. She looks at me, sees me looking at her. "Did Sarah throw up this morning?" she asks, sweetly.

"What?" I say.

"Did she throw up this morning?"

"I don't know," I say. "Why?"

"I did the morning I delivered," she says. "Of course, I did most every morning for nine months." She sounds proud. "The worst," she says, screwing up her face, "was ice cream." She turns a page. "Know why?"

I don't ask.

"Know why?" she says again.

"Why is that?" Kate says in monotone.

"Because it feels like cotton balls. Just like a whole box of Johnson & Johnson cotton balls coming up." She turns another page.

How much longer? Why didn't I look up the average labor time? Even if Sarah's okay, things can go wrong with the baby besides being premature. I keep thinking about what the Frasers said, Clem and his wife.

Met them back in the winter when sales were slow. January's always slow so that didn't bother me, but I thought it would be a good time to pack up Sarah and head for a warmer climate. Guys at the lot said we ought to go to Hawaii or Cancun or Las Vegas. Steve Brock said he and his wife went to Las Vegas and all she wanted to do was hear Wayne Newton, play the slot machines, and make love. Sounded good to me. So I called Sarah that morning from work and told her, "Pick out where ever you want to go. I'll call a travel agent and get us a deal."

But you know what she said? "The mountains!"

"It'll be cold," I said.

"North Carolina or Tennessee or Georgia. Doesn't matter," she said, her voice rising.

"It'll be cold," I repeated, "maybe icy."

"I don't care," she said and hung up.

By the time I got home for lunch she had our suitcases packed. "Let's go now, Jack," she said, throwing her arms around me. "We don't need reservations, let's just go." So we did.

We wound through the Georgia Mountains, past Dillard and Clayton and into North Carolina. Sarah wanted to stop at every store we came to. We'd go in, stay an average of twenty-seven minutes, then walk away empty-handed.

After the fifth store I got tired of going in so I bought a newspaper and waited in the car. "What are you looking for?" I asked her as she slid back in.

"A country store," she said.

"What are all these?"

"Stores," she said, looking at the road map, "but not country stores."

"Point us toward the next decent-sized town," I said, hoping for a restaurant and motel, maybe one with ESPN if I got lucky. I wanted to catch the North Carolina/Notre Dame game. I was depending on Sarah to read the road map. A mistake. I should know anybody who can translate the hell out of a hundred-year-old poem can't come down enough to read simple road numbers. Anyway, Sarah got us on this little winding back road that seemed to go on forever without getting anywhere.

Finally, I pulled over. "Give me the map, Sarah," I said, trying to sound patient. She flipped it at me, then shouted, "Look, Jack! up there around the curve. A little store." And before I could say "what?" she was out of the car and halfway to this boxy little weathered building.

It had a faded sign that read "Fraser's Store" nailed to a post on the porch. Sarah skipped up the steps without looking back. No one else was around. "Door's open!" she shouted. And in she went, me right behind her. No one inside either as far as I could tell. "Look, Jack," she said, pointing to the shelves.

"What?" I asked. Nothing remarkable. Just rows of Quaker Oats, baking soda, flour, salt — stuff like that. On the counter was a line of gallon jars. The first one had huge brownish-green pickles, that would put Joe's white cucumber to shame. The next one had eggs, boiled and shelled. The others had peppermint sticks, butterscotch drops, soft chewy-looking stuff, and red balls the size of fiberglass marbles.

"I'll bet those are fireballs," Sarah said, pointing to the last jar.

"You'd be right," a voice drifted through the air.

Sarah and I both jumped. In the back, next to a wood stove, sat an old man in overalls. His chair was reared back against the wall and his feet propped on the end of the counter.

"Clem Fraser," he said. "Pleased to meet ya." I nodded and stuck out my hand. Sarah didn't say anything.

"What ya need?" he asked, moving his feet and letting his chair settle on all four legs. "If ya need it, we got it. If ya just want it, we might not."

"May I look for a while," Sarah asked, already scanning the other wall.

"Course you can," he said. He reached behind his shoulder and banged on a door I hadn't noticed before. "Annie, come out here. We got some folks."

The door opened and out came a woman, I swear, who was the perfect bookend for old Clem. Her hair was grayish-brown and pulled back and pinned up. She wore a blue dress, shirtwaist, I think you call it. It was faded. "Well how do?" she said, looking from Sarah to me and back to Sarah, smiling all the time. Her voice was motherly. "What can I get for ya?"

"Fireballs," Sarah said.

"Fireballs?" the woman asked, eyeing Sarah up and down.

"Yes," said Sarah, poking her hands in her jeans, "a pound, please."

The woman shook her head. "I'll get em for ya, honey, but ya shouldn't be eating em in your condition." Sarah and I looked at each other. She had her shirttail out but she wasn't really showing. As a matter of fact, her own family didn't know she was pregnant.

"You with a child, ain't ya?" the woman asked, scooping out a load of red balls.

"Yes," Sarah said, "I am. But the fireballs aren't for me. They're for my aunt." The woman looked relieved.

"She must have one hell of a tough mouth," old Clem spoke up from the back.

"She does," I said.

The woman slipped the fireballs into a small brown bag. "You know you gotta be mighty careful what you do when you're aiming to have a baby." She looked Sarah straight in the eye. "You don't have no dog do ya?"

Sarah nodded, her green eyes wide.

"You not mean to him, are ya?"

"Oh, no," Sarah said. She looked to me for support.

"Not at all," I said.

The woman paused like she was considering whether or not to go on. "I know this girl, she weren't right to begin with, married Arthel Perkins, kin to Clem." She tipped her head in his direction. He nodded. "But not close. The whole time she was pregnant, she kicked Arthel's hound." She paused again. "When that girl had the baby, it come out hairy as a collie dog."

"Hairier," Clem said, "one ugly baby." He rocked back in his chair. "Talk was, Arthel might not be the father." He lowered his voice and directed his speech toward me, "Maybe some beast done got to her." He let his chair slam down.

"Arthel moved 'em away," the woman said, "for the shame of it all." She looked at Sarah. "So don't go kickin that dog of yourn no matter if he earns it or not."

"I won't," Sarah said. She looked pale.

"Course, there's some things go wrong can't nobody help," the woman went on. "You know what I'm speaking about, Clem." Clem nodded.

"She's talking about our own firstborn," he said. "Born with a veil over his head."

"A sign of God," the woman said, her voice cracking.

"If the devil don't get there first," Clem said. He stared at the back of his hands. "That devil sucked the breath right out of our baby boy. When I pulled the veil off his face, he was pretty as an angel. But he weren't breathing." Clem looked at the pine floor and paused. "But we done the right thing. Took the veil and sewed it up in a little quilt Annie made."

"It was red and white and had rams' heads on it," the woman said, looking beyond Sarah and me. "I made it for the baby. If he'd lived, he'd been a seer."

"We took it and our boy and buried 'em both up the hill aways. See?" Clem said, pointing toward the window, "right up there where the clouds come down at night."

I looked at Sarah. She was three shades paler, and her eyes were half-closed. The woman saw her too. "Dear Lord, Clem, we done scared this girl to death.'' They insisted she lie down on a little bed in the back room till she felt better. The woman went with her.

"Didn't mean to upset ya wife none," Clem said. "Annie'll talk to her, make her feel better. She's got powers. She's midwifed up and down these parts for some thirty odd years. Seen every kind of curse and other affliction that can come down on a little baby. She's sure seen a lot of misery. She's seen a heap of fine babies too. She'll make your missus better."

We stayed about an hour longer, the woman talking to Sarah, and Clem telling me mountain stuff. I'd have almost enjoyed the heat from the stove and hearing the old man talk if I hadn't been thinking about Sarah in there sick and about all those afflicted babies. When Sarah felt better, we drove on to Hendersonville and stayed the night. I left the phone book open to the number of a nearby hospital, just in case, and forgot all about the basketball game. Still it was a good trip and Sarah seemed refreshed back at home. We laughed a little about the fireballs but neither one of us mentioned the baby afflictions.

It's in my mind now though, right up front. Wonder what kind of "other afflictions" Clem was talking about? Hole in the heart, shriveled arms, blindness — Jesus! There's so much that can go wrong.

Who are all these people? It's too crowded in here! What in the hell are they shouting about? My baby? Somebody's baby?

I don't give a damn whether Sarah wants me with her or not. If it's my baby I've got a right to be there and if I'm the one who's there, by God, it'll be my baby!

SARAH

Sometimes you can't tell Jack anything. He had it all figured out to the month, to the day, probably even to the hour. I kept saying "earlier than you think." I didn't say how much earlier but I tried to prepare him.

That was after I made it to the sixth month. I began letting myself hope and from then on I didn't care if the whole world knew I was pregnant. Except Michael. I should have tried to find him, tell him about the baby. It would have been the right thing to do. But why start doing the right thing now? It's my baby regardless who the father is or who thinks he's the father.

Here it comes. Not too bad. I can stand it . . . try to re- lax . . . relax . . . relax . . . Over. I take a long breath and let it slip out slowly. Wonder if the baby feels contractions, his tight dark world shrinking around him.

I once read something about children whose skin can't tolerate light. Zero derma pigmentosa, I think. Mr. Medi-fact Andrew would know. They can't play outdoors in the sunshine. They live in constant dark, and they die early. I thought about my other babies like that. Jack said not to consider them babies the first few months just in case something happened. Something always did, but I still thought of them as my children, children of a dark play- ground.

"But this one, Dear God," I swear out loud, "even if it kills me, this one will see the light!"

"What's that? Mrs. Brighton?" the nurse asks. "Need some- thing?" She walks over to my bed.

"Nothing," I say. I try to read her name tag. Debbie something. "Nothing, Debbie," I say, "not yet."

This morning I knew I was close. I told Jack. He said it wasn't time, even double-checked his calendar. "False labor" he said in a voice uncomfortably close to Andrew's. As soon as he left for work, I drove straight to Dr. Fleming's office. He sent me to the hospital, but I came home first and called Donna. Her phone was busy. I usually drive whenever Donna and I go somewhere together but I couldn't by the time I reached her. She didn't ask me to. She spun her Honda in on two wheels, loaded me, then squealed out the driveway. She seem to enjoy the drama of it all.

The whole time she was talking. "Now Sarah, remember two things — breathe and relax. Breathe little short breaths like this — haa, haa, haa, haa, haa — during the pain." She looked straight at me the whole time she panted.

"I get it!" I shouted, "Watch where you're going!"

She glanced at the highway for an instant then back to me. "And relax. Breathe during the pain and relax in between. That way you save your energy for pushing."

"I thought you passed out after five minutes," I said, not feeling up to my usual patience with Donna.

"That was Andrew. He passed out. I went under. That's another thing to remember. If the pain gets too bad, make them give you dope. It's not like you'll be an addict or anything. Just tell them you want dope, and fast. Here we are," she said, turning into the parking lot somewhere between fourth and fifth gear. Donna stayed with me until I was admitted. She hurried out to make calls, then came back soon. That was about 11 this morning.

Jack didn't get here until 1 p.m. I assumed Donna had called him. As Jack would say, I "assumed wrong." He came in shouting at Donna, calling her I'm not sure what all. I was having a contraction at the time. But when it was over, I made them both leave. I was tired of Donna's chatting and I didn't want Jack to see me this way. Besides, I knew he was dying to look up the survival rate of a seven-month-old fetus. And too, I hear you can say just about anything when you're under Demeral or some other pain killers. I didn't want to take any chances. The nurse told me not to feel bad about the shouting, that families can act really strange at births and deaths. She said she'd seen a lot worse.

Must be about 2 now. There's a clock. Hard to see lying flat on my back. Wish I had my wrist watch. Haven't worn it since I stopped wearing rings. Micheal said I freed my hands. He didn't even have a pocket watch. Said he could tell the hour by the sun, and minutes don't matter that much when you're outside. That's what I'll do — imagine I'm outside looking at pretty things like sunsets and opal clouds and mountains. At least until the pain comes back.

Since last September I felt the pull of the mountains, calling me to come hide in the forests, to lose myself in the slopes and peaks and valleys.

In the summer it's too warm, too hazy to actually see the mountain ridge from our back yard. But you can see green hills rising toward morning fog. And sometimes after a rain when a little cold front moves through, you can see the long blue waves of mountains rise up behind the green hills.

By late November and December, I can see them almost every morning. And in the evening, if the clouds are just right, the sun lights the western sky with fiery pink, and the earth reaches up to meet it with layers of evergreen and cobalt blue. Sometimes I cry. It's so beautiful. And it pulls me so. Jack says, "Good God, Sarah, cry over something ugly, not beautiful." And I know such a sight should be calming but it sends my restlessness leaping out in flames. Like the morning I left with Michael. I've wondered if I would have gone in haze or fog too thick to see the mountains.

Whatever the pull, by last winter I was feeling it again so strong I could hear a voice calling me by name. I tried staying busy but the voice grew louder and louder. "Escape mechanism," Andrew would say, or "prenatal nerves" or "the voice of your own subconscious." Maybe so. I didn't tell Jack. But when he phoned out of the blue and asked me if I wanted to go to the mountains, I took it as the hand of Providence. Jack didn't actually say "mountains" but he did say "trip" and he let me do the choosing. Close enough.

It was spur of the moment, totally unlike Jack. Usually he has to research geographical climate, peak season, room rates, and exact distance before we do any traveling. But this time we just left, not even certain where we were going. We took our time — also uncharacteristic of Jack — and we drove back roads, stopped at lookouts and little mountain stores.

I kept searching for a country store, like Papa's, the one Mama and Aunt Kate grew up in. Mama had been on my mind since Aunt Kate's talk with me, not Mama as Mama but as Vivienne, a pretty girl longing for something she couldn't find at home.

Most of the stores were geared for tourists — rubber tomahawks, jointed plastic snakes, Taiwan baskets, ceramic bears. But we ran across one store, not as big as Papa's must've been, but the same atmosphere as Aunt Kate described. The Frasers owned it, Annie and Clem. They were what Byron and Shelley and Keats would have called "noble" in their simplicity and closeness to the earth.

Annie had a rhythmical quality about her. Her voice was sweet and sad and joyful all at the same time. She told stories about babies and animals and kinfolk, more mythical than real. I grew dizzy on her voice. So dizzy I almost fainted. She had me lie down on a bed in the back room of the store. The headboard was beautiful, burled walnut that shone almost golden in the light of the window. I rubbed it with my open palm.

"It's alive," Annie said. "When you fall asleep, the wood grain whirls all around you. But it moves back in place when you wake up." I stared at the swirls, thought I saw movement.

"You come up here for answers — didn't ya? — where everything is alive, where everything seems right," she said, touching her hand to my forehead. I nodded. "No fever. You just overwrought." She lifted her hand and stared into my eyes. I closed them but I could still feel her stare. "I can read eyes," she said. "Not just the seeing part but the lines around 'em. Can tell if you're lucky, how many babies you goin' have, if you got enemies, things like that. Even chilrun have lines, not so many but they have 'em." Her voice drifted in and out like the tones of a dulcimer.

"You got restless eyes," she said, "green like oak leaves in summer. Done caused you problems. You and ya lovin' ones."

"The baby," I said, not opening my eyes. "Tell me about the baby."

She ran her fingers around the outside corners of my eyes. "You lost babies already, ain't ya?" I nodded. "This baby goin' be special — if it lives."

"Boy or girl?" I asked.

"Hard to know the way ya carrin' so tight and all. Hope for a boy."

"Why?"

"If it's a girl, I hate to tell ya, she'll break your heart. Her pa's too."

"What if it's a boy?" I asked quickly.

"If it's a boy, he'll bring you and his pa together. You got problems?"

I didn't answer.

"Either way, this baby's special, you'll see it around the eyes." She squeezed my wrist.

126]

I fell asleep. A while later, Jack woke me and we left.

I didn't tell Jack what Annie had said. I wasn't even sure if she had actually said anything or I had dreamed it. But I thought about it all the next day as we wound through the Nantahala Forest. Jack had predicted ice, and he was right, as usual. Tree trunks and mountain laurel and sheets of granite all slick and shining with ice. Most of the time, he drove in second gear, a slow-motion, almost soundless ride through a land of silver. Annie's words seemed even more prophetic.

Wish she were here now. I can almost see her, feel her presence. "Annie?" I say out loud.

"I'm Debbie," the nurse says, her hand on my wrist. "You're doing just fine, Mrs. Brighton. But don't you want somebody from your family with you? Mr. Brighton or your sister? We'll make them behave," she adds with a smile.

"No," I say. "Not yet." I feel a new contraction. Rising white hot from the small of my back. Pressing upward straight through me. It's worse . . . getting worse . . . worse. How did Donna say to breathe? I grip the bed railing. Try to relax, I tell myself, it'll pass . . . relax . . . my brain whispers, relax . . . It passes. I catch my breath, wish I were somewhere else. For some reason I think about my family all seated around the Sunday dinner table.

The Sunday after our mountain trip, we had dinner at Donna's.

"Sarah, I want to hear all about your trip," Donna said right after the blessing. "Daddy, have some casserole and pass it on. It's Chinese. Real easy. You just put in some of those Chinese vegetables, they come in a can. And a can of chicken." She glanced at Andrew. "Only, I had to use tuna. Sent Andrew to the Dixie store, you know I always go, but I was doing Daddy's laundry." We both looked at Daddy. He was sniffing the casserole. He dipped out a spoonful and passed the dish to me.

"Andrew got tuna by accident." She looked back at Andrew. We all did. "Tell them why, honey." He didn't speak. "Because," she said stroking him on the arm like a child, "he saw the 'Chicken' part of 'Chicken of the Sea' and bought it! He didn't realize they were talking about fish!" Everybody laughed. Except Andrew. He made a weak attempt. "Then he forgot the water chestnuts. So I

[127

just used pecans. You know you can substitute. I forgot to write down chow mein noodles — that wasn't Andrew's fault — but I had a can of tater sticks on hand. They're just as crunchy." She passed the peas to Andrew. "Now tell me about your trip."

"Ice," Jack said. "All the way from Nantahala to this side of Brevard." He looked at me and smiled. "But we met an interesting couple, didn't we?" He pressed his knee against mine.

"They had a country store," I said, spooning a little casserole, as little as I thought I could get by with. "Aunt Kate, it must have been like Papa's — oiled wood floors, rows of huge glass jars, tools — nothing touristy." I passed the Chinese tuna to Jack.

"And a wood stove," Jack added. He looked at the casserole, then at Donna. She was zeroed in on his spooning hand. He dipped out a serving no larger than mine and passed the dish quickly to Kate. She waved it by and sent it to Andrew. Andrew graciously received it and made two grandiose scoops. Donna beamed. Daddy rolled his eyes.

"The Frasers," Jack said. "Annie and Clem Fraser, the mountain couple. They both spoke this thick mountain dialect. Andrew, you would have enjoyed that." Andrew was scraping tater sticks off his casserole. He looked guilty. "Mr. Fraser said he farmed a little too. His wife delivered babies."

"And she could read the lines around your eyes," I added.

"Now that's interesting," Donna said. "Don't skimp on the casserole. Law, I forgot the Jello salad. It's orange with carrots and pineapple. It's real pretty. I did it in a mold like Mama used to." Donna headed for the kitchen.

"Sure she didn't read palms?" Andrew said, reaching for a roll.

"She read eyes, lines around the eyes."

Andrew split the roll in two and pushed the casserole toward Charlotte. Charlotte pushed it toward Scarlet. "Guess she surmises the more lines, the older you are or the more ultraviolent rays you've been exposed to. A wrinkle-reader of sorts." He seemed pleased with himself. He loaded a blob of Chinese tuna minus the tater sticks onto his fork, smiled, and popped it into his mouth like he'd made a point. He chewed a few times then quit smiling.

"She didn't talk about age or sun," I said, feeling slightly annoyed. "She said even children have lines." Charlotte and Scarlet looked at each other. "She can tell how many children you've had, if you're lucky, if you have any enemies, things like that."

Donna came back to the table carrying a platter of Jello chunks. She set it in front of the twins. "Couldn't get it out of the mold in one piece," she said. "It'll taste just as good." Scarlet rolled a chunk onto her plate and pushed the platter toward Charlotte. Charlotte did the same.

"Did she do you, Sarah?" Donna asked. She looked at the casserole, three-quarters full. "Maybe it needs to set. Some dishes taste better the day after, lets their flavors mingle. Like Mama's vegetable soup." We all nodded. "We'll have it tomorrow." My side of the table nodded again. Andrew and the twins looked desperate.

"Did she do you?" Donna repeated, sliding her chair closer to the table.

"Do what?"

"Tell your fortune. I heard you saying something about reading eyes."

I looked at Jack. He was staring at me. "Not really," I said, "but she did seem to notice things."

"The man told me," Jack added quickly, "that neighbors came to his wife to find out when to plant."

Daddy perked up. "I used to know a man who could do that," he said. "Emmet, Emmet . . . I forget his last name. I was a little boy at the time. He could read the moon — the rings around it, its color, things like that. My own daddy wouldn't plant 'less Emmet gave him the go-ahead."

"Did he charge anything?" Andrew asked, lifting his eyebrows.

"Not that I recall," Daddy said, staring in the distance. "Course, we probably kept him in vegetables."

"Every culture," Andrew said, slipping into his lecture voice, "has its own brand of mystics and psychics, depending on what's important to them: winning battles, proliferating, farming. Most are fakes and most have a price."

"Like fortune cookies!" Donna said. "That reminds me — Wilene down at Holly's Hair and Then Some said that new Chinese restaurant out on the bypass is okay but they use too much MG."

"You mean monosodium glutamate," Andrew said.

"That's right, Andrew," she said, stroking his arm again, "but its initials are MG. And Wilene said if you don't take your fortune with you, they take that little slip of paper right off your plate and bake it up in another cookie. She's got the same one three times. It said, 'The fool only talks. The wise man only listens.' "

"Maybe there's some truth," Andrew said, looking straight at Donna.

"Maybe so," Aunt Kate added, looking straight at Andrew.

"Aunt Kate, I almost forgot," I said, "I brought something for you." I pushed back from the table, reached for my purse, and pulled out the small brown bag of fireballs.

Aunt Kate took the bag and carefully unrolled the end. Her face lit up and for an instant she looked like the little girl in the portrait with Mama. "Hot damn!" she said. Andrew looked at her hard and nodded toward the twins. She ignored him. "I haven't had any of these in forty years!" She popped one in her mouth.

"What are they?" Donna asked, straining toward our side of the table.

"Fireballs," Aunt Kate said. She looked around the table. Her eyes settled on Andrew. "Y'all want some? How about you, Andrew? Bet you didn't have these in Massachusetts." She stretched her arm toward him and shook the open bag.

Andrew looked suspicious. He peered in cautiously, then relaxed. "Jawbreakers," he said. "We called them jawbreakers and they came in fruit flavors."

"These are different," Aunt Kate said, rolling the ball with the tip of her tongue. "Try one." She smiled and shook the bag again.

Andrew looked around the table. We were all watching him. He reached inside the bag, selected one red ball, and slipped it into his mouth. He tucked the candy into his left cheek, smiled, and nodded at Kate. She was still rotating her fireball with her tongue. Andrew quit smiling. He shifted the ball to his right cheek. It looked like he was rubbing the inside of his left cheek with the tip of his tongue.

He reached for his tea glass. Half-full. He emptied it in one gulp. He shifted the ball again and searched the table.

"What you looking for, Honey?" Donna asked. She was folding her napkin into smaller and smaller squares.

"The pith-er," Andrew mumbled.

"The what?" Donna asked.

"The tea pith-er," Andrew said. Daddy was starting to make little noises, coughing-like noises but not exactly.

"Pit-cher, Andrew, we call it the pitcher. It's in the kitchen." Donna didn't make a move to get up.

Andrew stared at her, his eyes wide, they were starting to tear. "Plea-th, get it!" he tried to whisper, "now!"

Kate looked at her own glass. It was full. She kept her fireball rolling. Donna rose from the table, slower than usual, and headed for the kitchen. Andrew crammed his hand in his glass and trapped an ice cube. He threw it into his mouth. His nose was starting to run. He dapped at it with his napkin.

"You didn't spit out, did you?" Aunt Kate asked, suspicion in her voice.

Donna reappeared with the tea pitcher. "Why Andrew, you're almost out of ice," she said. She set the pitcher in front of him and whisked away his glass. "Get anybody anything while I'm up?"

"I-th!" shouted Andrew. Then he started chewing, more biting than chewing, like Bilo after fleas. He swallowed hard. Reached for Charlotte's glass, drained it and swallowed three or four more times. Then he opened his mouth and panted — "Haa, haa, haa, haa."

"Oh, Andrew!" Donna said. "You sound like you're in labor!" Andrew mumbled "fresh air" and rushed from the table. No one laughed, not until we heard the front door slam.

I start to laugh now just remembering. Another contraction stops me. You can make it, I tell myself. Make it. Make it. Make it. Make it . . . I'm as dry as Andrew must have been. Something in the shot they gave me or maybe I'm panting like Donna and Andrew.

"May I have some water?" I ask.

"Sorry, no water," Debbie answers with nurse-pleasantness, "but I'll get a moist towel and hold it to your face."

I close my eyes. Rest.

Another pain awakens me. Sharper . . . longer . . . longer . . . longer . . . like all the miscarriages clumped together. I try to separate from my body . . . float my brain up to the light . . . look down and watch myself. It doesn't work. Dear God, it hurts! The sound of pain rises in my throat. I grit my teeth, try not to cry out. I hear movement. A male voice, shouting. "Give her something! Can't you give her something?"

Debbie's words float in and out, "Better . . . not too sedated. . . better for both."

It eases. I open my eyes. Jack stands over me, pressed against the bedrails. He strokes my arm. "I'm here to stay," he says. "Don't argue with me, Sarah."

I start to open my mouth. Another contraction. From my soles to my scalp, pulling me in a ball. I grip the bars to keep from folding up, hold my breath, squeeze my eyes hard. I rock myself like a baby trying to fall asleep. Rock . . . rock . . . back . . . and forth . . . and back. I feel Jack's hand against my cheek. The bed begins to move. I open my eyes again. Jack holds on to the side.

"We're taking her," Debbie says, trying to pry Jack's hand loose from the rails.

"I'm staying with her," he says.

"Did you make arrangements?"

"I'm staying," he repeats.

Debbie looks from Jack to me, then back to Jack. "Okay," she says, an edge to her voice, "but you can't go like that. Wait here until I get back." She grabs the foot of the bed and starts to pull again. Jack holds on a second longer like he's in a tug of war. Then he lets go.

More pain. Both faces fade as the bed rolls into the hall. Light after light after light whirls above me. Another room. A huge circle of florescent light. So bright I can hardly keep my eyes open. Voices. People in green gowns, caps, masks. Nothing showing but eyes. Suddenly I want Jack, need Jack. I want to scream his name. More eyes rush in. Lean over me. Blue, deep blue. "Jack?" I say. He nods. A brown curl escapes from underneath the green cap. He squeezes my hand. I squeeze back. "You look silly," I whisper. He nods again. His eyes squinch up at the corners in a smile.

Another set of eyes hang over me. Brown! Dark as night! I panic. Michael's here! How did he know? I look at Jack. He doesn't seem to notice. "You're doing fine, Mrs. Brighton," the brown eyes say. I recognize the voice. Dr. Fleming.

I relax. But only for a second. Another contraction grips me, so strong I feel I'm being squeezed in two. I nearly sit up with the pressure. "Keep pushing, Mrs. Brighton," someone says. I close my eyes, catch my breath, and bear down with all my strength, with the energy of the universe ringing in my ears. Again and again.

"It's here!" a male voice shouts. A female voice cheers. Someone presses hard on my empty abdomen. I rest my head, afraid to open my eyes, afraid to hear any more.

A hand strokes my forehead, pushes back my wet hair. I look up with blurred vision. Blue eyes, bright as the sky, fanned out in a line like a geometric pattern, blue touching blue touching blue. I blink a few times and focus. Jack's eyes hold mine.

"Congratulations!" a voice shouts. I recognize Debbie. She lays a squirmy, wet, beautiful creature across my heart. "Mr. and Mrs. Brighton," she says, "you have a boy."

I look from the baby to Jack. Jack closes his eyes. His lashes glisten in the florescent light.

PART V

DEPARTURE

DONNA

Little Sammy's got the weirdest eyes. Sarah's baby. Not that he isn't beautiful. Samuel Joseph Brighton — that's what they named him. Brighton after Jack. Joseph after Daddy. I'm not sure where they got Samuel. Sarah said it was from Aunt Kate. Of course, Aunt Kate could have suggested a whole lot of men's names. But I don't remember a Samuel.

Sammy hadn't opened his eyes good until Andrew and I were guessing at the color. See, most babies start out with blue eyes. But after a while the color changes if it's going to be green or brown. Take my own Scarlet. Her eyes were clear blue, blue as Windex — and they stayed that way. But Charlotte's had these little gold flecks in them. They turned brown like Andrew's.

Andrew and I couldn't agree on what color Sammy's eyes would be. I said they'd stay blue. His left eye was as blue as Scarlet's. But Andrew said brown because of the other eye. We were both right. And wrong. One stayed blue and the other turned brown, pale brown like a hazel nut. The pediatrician says they're rare, but they both work. Sarah thinks they're wonderful. Those eyes. Sometimes I don't understand her way of thinking. But then again, I'm understanding more than I used to.

Sarah's cowboy is back. The veterinarian. He comes riding up to Aunt Kate's farm this morning, almost a year ago to the day Mama died. He's pulling a horse trailer. And if my eyes don't deceive me, Sarah's horse is in it. I was over there at the farm giving Aunt Kate some of Daddy's garden stuff so I wouldn't have to fool with it anymore. He's about to drive me crazy. Andrew doesn't understand. He just says, "Quit doing so much for him. You've got your own family to think about." See, that's it. Andrew thinks I should be doing things for HIM instead of Daddy. I'm dog tired of doing for BOTH of them. Sarah would understand but she's so busy with little Sammy she doesn't half listen. That leaves Aunt Kate.

But getting back to the vet, I'm pulling out when he comes riding up. I have to admit he looks good. Dark and kind of mysterious, a full beard, and a Charlie Daniels' type hat shading his eyes. I'm beginning to see what moved Sarah. I watch him in my rear-view mirror.

I haven't told anybody about seeing him. Not even Andrew. I don't want to hear his analysis of the situation. He analyzes my family all the time like they're some kind of wack-O's. He should study his own relatives, the Websters. They're plenty strange, let me tell you. He's got this aunt that lives with his mama, Aunt Ruth. She swallows toothpaste water. I've seen her do it. The stuff most people spit out, she swallows. And she walks sprattle-legged up and down the halls where they live. The first time I saw her do it, I thought she was deformed. Andrew said she walks that way to keep from wearing a path on the carpet. Is that not weird? And then there's Mrs. Webster, Andrew's mother. The very first time she had dinner with my family, it was right before the wedding, she asked for unsweetened tea. Mama was in the kitchen, thank goodness. I told Mrs. Webster we didn't have any made up without sugar. So she asked for water to "thin it down a little." I was embarrassed to death until Aunt Kate spoke up real fast. She said, "Around here our tea is like our men, sweet and strong."

See why I don't tell Andrew about Sarah's vet? And to be honest, I enjoy knowing things Andrew doesn't. Like with Aunt Kate's new boyfriend.

Andrew didn't find out about that till Sunday dinner. It had been going on almost a week by then. That was July, already hot as August. Thought I'd have a light dinner — just ham, potato salad, rolls, corn on the cob, tomatoes, blueberry pie with vanilla ice cream. Sarah and Jack brought little Sammy. He was about three months old then. That cute stage when they have a little more backbone and aren't so jerky. Scarlet and Charlotte made a big fuss over him and wanted to hold him but Daddy wouldn't let them. He held Sammy the whole time. Sarah seemed comfortable enough, but Jack watched Daddy like a hawk.

I have to tell you, Daddy's really blossomed since this spring. With little Sammy around and his own vegetable garden, he came back to life. It was good to see him digging around in the dirt again, burying seeds, watching them break, grow, leaf out. He gets real satisfaction sharing with all of us and having me cook up his vegetables for Sunday dinner. There's just one thing about Daddy's garden I didn't like — I guess you could say I've come to hate. That's canning and freezing all that stuff Daddy hauls into the kitchen. I don't see how Mama stood it. I don't mind boiling a little of this and bagging a little of that. But, my Lord! Daddy comes dragging these bushel baskets full of green or orange or yellow stuff and says "Donna Jean, this needs to go into the freezer today," or "Donna Jean, these would make some fine pickles," or "Do what you want with these. I just grow 'em, but I sure hate to see 'em go to waste."

Getting back to the "subject at hand," as Andrew would say, it was Sunday dinner in July before he knew about Kate's new boyfriend. Andrew kept looking around the table. "What you need?" I asked.

"Kate," he said.

"What? You need Aunt Kate?" I couldn't help laughing. I looked at Sarah and she laughed too. Daddy was busy watching Sammy and Jack was busy watching Daddy.

"I mean — where is Kate?" he said. "She hasn't missed a Sunday dinner in over a year."

Sarah and I quit laughing but we couldn't help smiling. For just an instant, I heard the theme to "Bonanza" humming around in my head.

"What is it?" Andrew asked. "What are you two smiling about?"

"Sarah, how about helping Daddy to some ham and potato salad since he's all tied up with Sammy." I pushed the rolls toward Andrew, "Why don't you start these?"

"I always start the rolls," he said. "You don't have to say that every Sunday." I thought I saw that little muscle in his jaw twitch. He reached for a roll and tore it in two with more force than was necessary. "Now what's your and Sarah's secret about Kate?"

"New boyfriend," I said, helping myself to a roll. I tore mine in two, gently so as not to ruin the consistency, just like I was tearing sliced bread. The halves separated perfectly. It's all in the wrists. Then I spread on a little butter. Actually it's fake butter that's fake margarine, all whipped and colored so that it looks better than the real thing. They say it's better for you. I'm not so sure.

"New boyfriend?" Andrew asked.

"Yes," I said. But I was watching Daddy scrape and saw his ham, one-handed, with one of Mama's good silverware knives. They're pretty but not very sharp. "What you doing, Daddy?"

"What's it look like?"

"Like you're trying to cut your ham into teeny-tiny baby-size pieces."

Jack looked like I'd just confirmed his worst suspicions. "Sammy can't eat table food," he said.

"How do you know?" Daddy said, squashing a potato cube with his fork. "Has he tried any?"

Before Jack could shout "No!" or maybe right at the same time, Daddy poked a spoonful of mushed-up potato into Sammy's mouth.

Jack shot back from the table and made an attempt to rise, but Sarah clamped down on his shoulder pretty hard. Sammy was smiling.

"He likes my potato salad," I said, trying to lighten things up a little. "Sarah, I'll give you my recipe."

Sarah smiled, but Jack didn't. "That won't be necessary, Donna Jean," he said. Then he looked straight at Daddy and in the same voice he used for "Donna Jean" he said, "No ham!"

"Where'd she meet him?" Andrew said.

"Who?" I said. "Have some potato salad and pass it to the girls."

"Where did Kate meet her new boyfriend?" he said, trying to shake a blob of salad off the spoon. It came loose and spattered just a little. "The Wayfarer Lounge?" he asked, dabbing at his tie with the napkin.

"Floyd's Feed and Seed," I said. "It'll wash out." But I was more concerned with getting Daddy and Jack back to eating than Andrew's old tie. "Sarah, have an ear of corn and pass the rest to Jack. I couldn't find those little handles you poke into the ends of the cob. We used to use those when we were little. Remember, Sarah? Mama must have thrown them out. Daddy, have you seen them?"

Daddy was trying to eat his corn with one hand like a chicken leg. "What?" he said. Little bits of yellow stuck to his chin.

"Those little pointy things Mama used to stick into the ends of the cob."

He shook his head. Corn bits fell off his chin and back into his plate.

"Go on," Andrew said. His lips moved but his jaw was clenched.

"She used them so Sarah and I wouldn't burn our fingers," I said. "Or more likely get them greasy with butter and wipe them on our clothes." I smiled just remembering.

"Not about the corn skewers," Andrew said, making "skewers" sound almost nasty, "about Kate's new boyfriend." I was sure I saw the muscles twitch that time.

"Aunt Kate met him at the feed store. She said he was driving this custom-type truck. Real big and nice. She called it a Dooley."

Jack stopped watching Daddy. Daddy stopped watching Sammy. Almost in unison they said, "a what?"

"A Dooley," I said. "You know, like hang down your head Tom Dooley."

"She probably meant a 'dually,' " Jack said. Daddy nodded.

"What did it have on it?" Daddy asked. He's always interested in trucks.

"I don't know anymore about the truck itself," I said. Daddy looked disappointed. "Just the contents," I added. "Kate said he was pulling a trailer with a llama in it."

"A llama?" Andrew said. "Are you sure she said 'llama'?

I nodded.

"Michael Jackson has a llama," Scarlet said, pushing the potato salad bowl toward Charlotte.

"Is that Fred Jackson's son, out near the fire station?" Daddy said. "I thought he joined the Navy."

Scarlet looked at Charlotte. They both squeezed their lips together and blew out their cheeks. Just like Sarah and I used to do. I stared them down. "No, Daddy," I said, "that's a different Jackson."

"Good potato salad," Sarah said. She sounded surprised. "Aren't llamas like camels?" she asked.

"I don't know," I said, "but Aunt Kate said he has a whole ranch of llamas in Washington.

"They're ruminants related to the camel," Andrew said, "mostly used for pack animals, hiking and camping."

"Pack animals in Washington?" I said. "Who'd want to go camping around the White House unless you were protesting something."

"Probably the state of Washington," Sarah said.

"Whatever," I said, "that's all I know about Aunt Kate's new boyfriend." I knew he was staying out at the farm with her but I didn't want to say so in front of the twins. I helped myself to an ear of corn and passed the dish to Andrew.

"This reminds me," Andrew said, reaching for some corn, "of something I read in *National Geographic*."

"About llamas?" Sarah asked.

"No, about corn. Actually about grits." Here we go again, I thought, nasty comments about grits. I looked at Sarah and she rolled her eyes. Jack would have joined in with Andrew — he doesn't like grits either — but he was watching Daddy eat ham.

"Grits," he said in his lecture voice, "aren't really of Southern origin but rather a food of the ancients." He paused a moment, to let that sink in, whatever it meant, then went on, "It was an Aztec breakfast, discovered by some Mexicans in the 1500's." How does he do it? — I'm thinking — store all those little bits of dates that don't have a thing to do with anything that matters as far I can tell, and on top of that forget our anniversary?

That would have been all right, though, except he added, "When someone calls you people a 'grit,' they're really calling you an 'Aztec.' " Then he told us something truly remarkable. "Yellow grits come from yellow corn," he said, gesturing toward the ear in Daddy's hand, "and white grits come from white corn." I looked at Sarah. She had her lips squeezed together and her cheeks blown out just like the twins a minute ago. I probably would have too except I'd about had it with Andrew's little education tidbits. More than fifteen years of them can drive you nuts.

Then Daddy spoke up, "That reminds me, Donna Jean. The corn needs to be put up tomorrow. Won't wait. We'll start on it first thing in the morning."

Damn! — I thought — Damn you both and all your old corn! I almost said it out loud except for the twins. Sarah looked at me sympathetic-like. She knew what I was thinking. Then I felt kind of guilty. Donna Jean, I said to myself, here's poor old Daddy finally getting over Mama's death. Think of all he's done for you.

Then I thought about Andrew, sitting there eating a bite of ham and a bite of potato salad and a bite of roll and a bite of corn, in that order over and over. No matter how aggravating he gets, I should still love him. I mean you couldn't just quit loving somebody after living with them this long. Could you?

I decided it was just me. I needed a change. I started thinking about make-overs again. Lately Andrew had hardly noticed I was alive and the twins had started referring to Andrew and me as "the fossils." Andrew said that was just teenage slang and a natural way to "snip the bonds of parenthood." But I still didn't like it. I told them I'd be snipping allowance, laundry, and anything else that stuck out if I heard that "fossils" stuff again.

Getting a make-over in this town was tougher than I thought. We don't have any *Glamour*-type experts unless you count what Holly gets from her cousin in California. She's a beautician too. Sometimes she sends Holly samples of the latest beauty product out there, like anti-aging eye gel or tan enhancer. Andrew says they're made from bull semen and embryo fluids. But I don't believe that for one minute. Holly says she doesn't either. We both tried the samples and that was it for make-overs.

Then a few months back a new cosmetic store opened in town. They ran a coupon in the newspaper that said "free makeup lesson." That's it, I thought, so I clipped the coupon, washed my face, and went. The only person there was this salesgirl, not much older than the twins, who looked like she had on every eyeshadow in the store. Her makeup instruction consisted of pulling out a box of half-used samples, handing me a mirror, and saying, "Keep trying till you find what you like. That's what I do."

I might have given up if Holly's cousin hadn't come for a visit. While she was here, she set up shop at Holly's Hair and Then Some. Her name was Barbra, not Bar-ba-ra like I thought at first. She preferred Barb. Sounded too much like wire to me, but Holly called her Barb so I did too. Barb offered free make-overs, hoping, of course, to sell makeup. The way she talked you could tell she was from California. And she really knew her business. She started with cleanser, then clarifier, followed by astringent that she said "snaps the pores." Barb spread foundation with this little pie-wedge sponge. She said, "Never the fingers." She also used sponges because they were disposable. "In LA," she said, lifting one eyebrow, "you NEVER re-use a sponge."

Barb used two kinds of blush on me to bring out the "sharpness in my cheekbones." And the whole time she was telling me how pretty I was and with the right makeup I could look ten years younger. I bought the package. All $76 worth. It was a starter kit and had all the cleansers and brushes and makeup in a pretty little blue carry case I could take on trips. Not that Andrew and I travel much unless you count Myrtle Beach every other summer.

I planned to tell Andrew about my make-over as soon as he noticed how different I looked. I was going to show him the kit and tell him what Barb said. But not the price. I considered that a beauty secret. That was my plan until I came home. Know what he said? "You look different around the mouth. Your lips are swollen. Have you been eating oranges?"

Still the make-over was a good experience because I started thinking about going into business myself. "Donna's Make-over Magic." I imagined a small shop with wall-to-wall photographs. I'd put the "befores" on one side and the "afters" on another. Then waiting customers could try to match them or pick out a look they especially liked.

I told Holly and she said she'd give me a corner in the shop. But she said I'd have to get a certificate or license or something to show I know my stuff. Something to hang on the wall in one of those black frames like Andrew has in his office. There's a school in Atlanta I could go to. Holly gets ads from it all the time.

I could take that old dressing table Mama meant to refinish and do it myself or maybe just give it a coat of glossy white paint. I could dig out the Polaroid camera Andrew gave me for Mother's Day a couple years back, and I could "snap" the befores and afters right on the spot.

I'd accept walk-ins at first. Holly doesn't usually. She makes them an appointment and sends them right back out the door. Except for people from the campground down the road. She gets a good many customers just passing through. Some may want make-overs. I've met some really interesting people from the campground. Like this man who invented blowing up buildings so they fall straight down instead of exploding all over the place. He came in with his wife. While Holly did her hair, he told us about places he'd been — New York, Minneapolis, Denver — just about everywhere somebody wanted something big, blown down. He was on his way from Florida to Nevada. I asked him if he was going to blow up a casino. He said no, but he might shake down a slot machine or two. He was funny but he had an accent.

He gave Holly and me his business card, like we might have something to blow up. When they got ready to leave, we went out to see their camper. He called it a "travel home" and he was right. It must have been 30 feet long. Biggest one I've ever seen. Holly too.

That's another reason I want my own make-over business — to meet interesting people. It's sort of like traveling with them when they tell you where they've been or where they're going. The thing is, if I go down to this school in Atlanta, I'll have to leave Andrew and the girls and Daddy for two whole weeks. Andrew's so busy on that research project of his and the twins have to go to music and ballet and the mini-mall. Then there's Daddy.

That's what's been holding me back. But, you know, the more I think about it, the more tempting it sounds. I could cook up some meals and freeze them for while I'm gone. My pizza casserole, some hamburger patties, French toast — they all freeze well and taste good later if you defrost and heat them up right. I could fix some for Daddy too. The laundry might be a problem. Of course, the girls could do it if they just take their time and separate the colored stuff from the darks and whites. Daddy could take his to the cleaners. He probably won't do it, but that's up to him.

If I tell Andrew about going to Atlanta and taking a course, he'll try to talk me out of it. He'll come up with some other career move that will be more — I can hear him now — "financially feasible." Maybe I'll leave a note saying where I am and that I'll be back in two weeks. Or I could just go.

Like Sarah did. Wonder how she did it. I was too mad to ask her when she first came home. Then later when it looked like she'd be staying with Jack, it didn't seem so important. But it does now. With me feeling this way and her vet back and all. Wonder if she'll leave again. Take Sammy and the horse and just ride off. I've got to talk to Sarah. Ask her how she got the courage to leave the first time. And if she'll do it again.

AUNT KATE

I knew this day would come. She'd have to face him eventually.

I tried to prepare Sarah. I didn't say anything at the hospital. I waited until she was home and had her strength back. Then I went to see her.

"Door's open," she yelled from the nursery. She held Sammy on her arm, his head in the crook of her elbow, and dipped him in a small plastic bath tub. The stub of his umbilical cord protruded, a reminder of our connection to other animals.

She turned her head toward me, "Hi, Aunt Kate," then quickly back to the baby. "Don't want to get his belly button wet," she said. "He loves the water." She reached for a towel and in one swirl bound Sammy to her arm, then grabbed a diaper and little shirt. "We'll sit in the den while I dress him."

I chose a chair opposite the couch and watched Sarah. I could almost see Vivienne. I remembered her boiling all those diapers on top of the stove. She'd fish them out one by one with a wooden spoon, rinse them two or three times, then hang them on the clothesline. Sometimes I'd help. Joe bought her a washing machine when Donna came along. "Didn't have those plastic diapers when you were a baby," I said.

"I meant to use cloth," Sarah said, lifting Sammy's little butt by his feet and sliding a Pampers underneath it. "They're hard to find now. Cloth diapers." She lifted him to her chest, his head against her neck. He seemed content. She sat back and relaxed.

I took it as an opening. I drew a breath, let it out slowly, and said, "You've got to tell him."

"Tell who what?" Sarah said. Her green eyes widened then narrowed as though I'd flashed the light switch off and on. She turned her face from me to Sammy.

I said the word she'd carefully avoided for the past six months — "Michael."

"Tell him what?" she said in monotone. I could see the muscles in her arm tense. Sammy wiggled.

"Cut the crap!" I said. "You're in the same fix your mama was. Vivienne lived in fear of David showing up. Maybe more in hope than fear. That's the last thing she'd want for you. You've got to face Michael, tell him about his baby, and put it behind you, one way or the other."

She hesitated for a moment. "I don't know where he is," she said, "and besides," more defiance in her voice than I'd ever heard, "Sammy may not be his."

"Bullshit!" I said. "Sarah, I didn't come here to butt in your business. I just don't want to see Sammy in the same situation as you, growing up feeling something isn't right but not knowing what the hell it is."

"Jack is a good father," Sarah said, her voice starting to crack, "Sammy won't feel like I did. I won't let him!" She struggled to control her face. "I won't let him," she repeated.

I left.

We didn't talk again for a couple of months. At Sunday dinners Sarah was polite but that was all. And, hell, I'd had my say. But it hurt. She was like my own daughter and I felt cut off from my last bit of kin. Maybe she did too because one night she called and asked to come over "to visit," she said.

She brought a six pack of Bud. I had plenty but I didn't say so. I pulled off two and stuck the rest in the fridge.

"It's just June, and dear God, it's already hot," Sarah said. She slid the can across her temple, then held it to her neck.

"I've seen it hotter," I said, "but not much." I took a pull. "Jack keeping Sammy?"

She nodded. I expected a front-room conversation, so that's where we settled. She took several drinks, almost gulps. Her eyes swept the room. She looked at me and smiled. "Aunt Kate, you ought to date somebody in the air-conditioning business."

"That's an idea," I said, not altogether kidding. "Hell, I ought to date somebody!" I reached for my cigarettes. Lit up. "My only vice," I said. "Just one left."

"And baiting Andrew."

"Two, only two vices left," I said, "neither of which I plan to give up." We both laughed. Then we stopped and turned up our cans almost in unison.

"Ready for another?" I asked.

"I shouldn't," she said.

"That's not what I asked."

"Ready," she said.

When I came back, Sarah was staring at the mantelpiece. "I want to explain," she said without looking at me, "why I don't want Michael to know about Sammy." I popped the fresh can and handed it to her. She ran her finger around the rim, then took a drink.

"Aunt Kate, I loved Michael more than any man I've known." She pushed her hair back from her forehead. It was damp. "I still do in some ways. But the truth is I was planning to leave before I heard about Mama." Her voice shook. She took another drink. "And it wasn't because I was pregnant." She traced an initial on the can. I wondered whose.

"Before I left," Sarah said, wiping away the wet initial, "I felt like an old photograph, black-and-white turned gray, one that had been left in the sun too long. Sarah Crawford Brighton was fading, fading, until almost nothing was left. It wasn't Jack's fault — but that's the way I felt. Then Michael came along in living color. Like all outdoors. I was a teen again, giddy in love." She smiled and for a minute I saw her as seventeen again, auburn hair streaking behind her as she galloped Ulysses. "A real fantasy," she said.

"Contradiction in terms."

"Real fantasy? Maybe so, but Michael was romance — horses, log cabins, sunsets, opal skies. I took off like an airplane, higher on life than I'd been in twenty years, able to see so much more of it." Sarah stared into the fireplace as though she saw a flame. She took a pull on her beer. Then another.

"The thing is . . . "

"The down side," I said, finishing her sentence, "the crash." She looked surprised. Then studied the sweat on the can and nodded.

"Michael wouldn't let me stay close to him — not emotionally. He never even told me he loved me. I know he did at times, I could see it in his eyes. But he wouldn't say it. And every time he was especially tender, there'd be a week or so of distance." She stretched out her hand and scooped through the air as though she were retrieving a memory. "Like in Tennessee. I loved the mountains so much I didn't want to leave. Michael loved it there too, at first. We even planned our own cabin, drew it out on butcher paper — one big room with a river-rock fireplace, a kitchen of pine, a stained-glass window high over the bed. He wanted to find the perfect tree for our bed, have it cut into lumber then build it himself.

"One morning I woke up to find him packing. I asked him where he was going. Without turning around he said, "Heading west." I sat up in bed, pulled the sheets into a cocoon around me. I clutched a corner of the blanket like a child. I watched him cram things into a suitcase, searching my memory for some clue I must have missed. Then he looked me in the face, his dark brown eyes glazed over. Know what he said, Aunt Kate?"

I shook my head, but she wasn't looking in my direction.

"He said, 'You can come if you want.'" Sarah sat still, both hands cupped around her beer, as though she were back in that Tennessee bed.

148]

She straightened up, lifted her chin, and swept back her hair. My Sarah again. "I should have learned then," she said, "but I was so dependent on him for love and beauty and feeling alive that I went with him. Once we reached Texas he transformed back into the Michael I loved. Neither of us had been that far West so we were constantly amazed at the sights. Windmill after windmill, dust storms thicker than night, armadillos, prairie dogs. For a while I was glad I'd stayed with him, even felt heroic in a sense. But then the crash came again — a whole series of crashes. Michael would start to talk about feeling guilty for what we did to Jack. He'd ask me didn't I miss my family. Then he'd always finish by telling me he was just naturally a loner and always would be. I never knew if he was sincere or trying to make me feel bad enough to leave." She drained her can and grimaced again. "Up and down, up and down like a damn yo-yo! A Goddamn yo-yo!"

"Hurt like hell, didn't it?" I said, finishing off my beer. She nodded, the pain still in her eyes. "You're lucky," I added.

Her eyes widened. I let her think about that while I went for the last of her six-pack. "What do you mean, I'm lucky?" she said, a slight irritation in her voice. She took the beer.

"Pain," I said, "is a great balancer. It helps you get over memories, not bad memories but good ones, so good they can kill you." I opened the can and drank. Sarah stared at me. "I had painful memories with all my lovers," I said, "except Sammuel Harrison." I wiped a drip from my chin.

"Everything I remembered about him was good — his eyes, his hands, the way he touched me, the way he made me feel. Then he left — that's the only pain, terrible for sure but nothing I could really connect to him. I've wished a thousand times I had followed him, hung around long enough to see his meanness, or faults, or at least ordinariness. Instead of making him a god in my mind."

"Maybe you're right," she said. "But it's 'academic' as Andrew would say, because I won't see Michael again."

"Don't count on it," I said.

"It's been a year, Aunt Kate. No calls, no letters, no nothing." I couldn't tell if it was relief or sorrow in her voice.

"He's most certainly moved on by now, probably two or three times, found some other woman who dotes on his good moods and endures his bad ones."

"Sorry you left with him in the first place?" I asked.

"No," she said without hesitation. "I'm sorry about Mama and for what I did to Jack. But I had to save myself."

[149

"And now, Sarah?" I asked, "are you saved?"

She didn't answer. She bottomed out the beer and frowned at the can. "God, I hate that last swallow!"

"That's what Tennyson called 'drinking life to the lees.'"

She set the can down carefully as though it wasn't empty. "I'm not exactly Ulysses," she said, then smiled, "but he's got a point." She touched her hand to her chest.

"Still breast-feeding?" I asked.

"Yes," she said, "and I'm about due." She rested her head against the couch and closed her eyes.

"I'll drive you home."

"I can drive," she said but she didn't open her eyes. "Besides, I'm in the Cutlass. What'll I tell Jack?"

"Tell him it wouldn't start."

"I hate lying to him." Her words hung in the air. Her eyes popped open and for a minute I thought she might cry.

But I couldn't help laughing. "Sarah Crawford Brighton, since when did you become so honest!"

She started laughing too, soft at first, then deeper and louder until we both were holding our stomachs like we might get sick. "Dear God," Sarah shouted between fits, "I love you, Aunt Kate. You're the only one . . . "

"I know," I said, cutting her off short before she could get teary-eyed. I wanted to hear her laughter, so much like Vivienne's. I steered her to the Blazer and drove her home, more giggling now than laughing. "Good night," I told her. "Don't worry about Jack. He may not sleep well tonight, but you and Sammy will."

On the drive home, under the cool blaze of the moon, I thought about what Sarah had said. That part about Michael being a loner. She bought it and maybe he believed it too. But it's a crock. It's just a cheap way to avoid entanglements and separations. I ought to know, I've used it for two Goddamn years now. I'm not a bit better off. At least with entanglements there are risks, excitement, highs and lows. With this there's just one long monotonous "me."

I was still in that frame of mind the next day when I set out to wash my car. Somebody had run over the end of my hose where the nozzle screws on, Donna I think — she comes out here a good bit now. When I turned on the faucet, water shot up my arm and into my face. Soaked me. To the bone. And I was pissed. I didn't even go inside and change. I just headed out to Floyd's Feed and Seed to buy a new hose.

150]

There I stood, in a foul mood staring at the hose display, when I heard somebody say, "Who's the lady in the wet T-shirt and tight-fitting jeans?" He said the last part like Conway Twitty. Then I heard Floyd say, "That's Kate McMahan, but she's no . . . " I spun around before he could finish. Or maybe he did finish and I didn't hear what he said because leaning on the counter next to Floyd was the best looking man I'd seen in years, maybe eons. About eight or ten inches taller than me, salt-and-pepper hair, steel gray eyes, and a body like Adonis, a fifty-ish Adonis. Best of all, he was staring straight at me.

"Kate, this is Charlie Buchanan," Floyd said. "He raises llamas." I forced my eyes from Charlie to Floyd. Floyd's a cut-up, so I waited for the punch line. It didn't come.

"I really do," Charlie said, reading my mind. This is dangerous, I thought to myself. He seemed to read that too. He lifted his eyebrows and smiled. "My ranch is in Washington," he said, "but I have one of my llamas with me, outside. Taking her to Georgia." He shifted his weight from one boot to the other. Suede boots. I love suede, but I tried not to think it. He winked. "Want to see?"

"You're not pulling my leg, are you?" I said, then attempted my best smile. The thought about the leg was not unpleasant. He motioned and I followed him out to the parking lot. He stopped beside a rig that would have had Joe and Jack talking for days. It was a silvery-blue Chevy truck, chrome-trimmed, with running boards, an extended cab, and dual rear wheels. Behind it was a matching gooseneck trailer, sleek as a bullet. Washington tags read LLAMA 1.

"Like it?" Charlie said with a little-boy smile. I nodded. I peeked inside the trailer. There stood what appeared to be two animals in one. A giraffe's head and neck on a sheep's body with extra long legs, all bound together in creamy white fur.

"Snow White," Charlie said, "meet Kate." Snow White turned to look. I expected a silly mug, but her face was beautiful — a face of curves, delicate rounded nostrils, ears shaped like Ss, big round eyes with sweeping lashes — all balanced on a small, delicate head. "Pretty thing, isn't she?" Charlie said.

"Yes," I answered, still surprised at my own thoughts. I turned to Charlie. He was looking straight into my eyes. I turned away and looked back at the trailer. "You're hauling all the way from Washington?" I asked. He nodded. "Nice trailer and all," I said, "but doesn't she need to get out and exercise some?"

[151

"I stop several times a day," he said, stroking Snow White's neck, "unload her and lead her around. Then at night she and I go for a run."

"Where?" I asked, trying to picture man and llama out for a jog in the countryside or along the highway. Either way, around here they'd cause a wreck or at least a good story or two.

"Lately, it's been around the motel wherever I'm staying. We get a lot of funny looks, especially from people coming out of the motel lounge."

I could imagine the talk down at the Wayfarer, "I just saw some man chasing a giraffe. No, an albino deer. No, it was the biggest damn poodle I ever saw!" The thought made me smile. Charlie smiled too. I didn't know if he was reading my mind again or just smiling at me.

The sun was hot but a little breeze stirred. It felt good against my skin. I looked from Charlie to Snow White then back to Charlie. "Why don't you bring her out to my farm," I said, trying to sound casual. "What's kept in horses and cattle ought to keep in a llama."

"Most likely," Charlie said, sliding into the cab without hesitation. I started toward the Blazer. "Ride with me and lead the way," he said. "We'll get your car later."

I stood there a minute and asked myself, what are you doing, Kate? Riding off in this big shiny dually with a perfect stranger? An answer didn't come so I hopped onto the running board and slipped in beside him. As Charlie drove, I studied his profile. Strong chin. Smooth like he'd just shaved. My fingers itched to find out. He seemed happy and tense at the same time like he was going to his high school prom. He kept his eyes on the road most of the trip to the farm, but occasionally he turned toward me as though he thought I might disappear.

We stopped at the barn, unloaded the llama, and led her through the hallway to the back lot. Long time since a man like this had set foot in this barn, too long, I thought as we walked.

Snow White seemed happy to have some real space, grass underneath her feet, pine trees over her head. As she walked around surveying her surroundings, I was amazed at how graceful she moved. We watched her together for a while without talking. At that moment I felt more peaceful than I'd been in years, or ever. I almost hated to break the tranquility but finally I said, "How about lunch?" Charlie smiled and nodded.

I fried bacon, sliced one of Joe's Big Boy tomatoes, and made us a couple of sandwiches. When I poured the ice tea, I noticed my hand shaking. Get a grip, I told myself, calm down, you've fed a dozen men in this very kitchen. I laid out two napkins, then two more in case the tomatoes got sloppy, and called Charlie inside.

"Wish I had more in the way of lunch," I said, thinking I should have had him stop at the Dixie store or Bi-Lo on the way home and gotten ham or sliced chicken. I'd have even welcomed Donna's potato salad. "I don't keep that much just for me."

"This is fine," he said, biting off a corner. His hands almost hid the sandwich. Bacon stuck out between his fingers. He chewed, swallowed, and took a big swig of tea. "Good tea," he said, "sweet and strong, the way I like it." He looked into my eyes. "I know what you mean. I don't keep much just for me either."

"Just for me" kept ringing in my ears. "You live alone?" I asked, trying to sound casual again.

He nodded and took another bite.

"Who's minding the ranch?" I asked, double-checking on the "alone" business.

"Herdsman," Charlie said, wiping his mouth with the napkin. "First time I've left the ranch for any length of time, but he'll do okay. He usually delivers the stock, but I wanted to take this trip myself."

"Why?" I asked. "Seems like an awfully long haul."

"That's why," he said, "because it is a 'long haul.'" Guess I looked confused. He paused a minute as though he were carefully selecting his next words. "Kate McMahan, do you believe in fate?"

I thought a minute or two. "I don't know," I said, "seems like some things just go wrong without your being able to do anything about them."

"Not bad fate," he said, "I mean good fate."

"Don't think I've ever seen such an animal," I said.

Charlie laid both hands, palms down, on the table. He leaned forward. "I've felt something drawing me," he said, "for the past couple of years now. I'm not sure what to call it except 'fate.' When this trip across the country came up, I felt that this may be it, the way to find whatever it is." He sat back and pushed his hands in his pockets. "Do you understand?"

"I'm not sure," I said, trying to keep a clear head. But before I could think much more about it, Charlie was on his feet.

"When's the last time you walked your fences?" he asked.

"Too long," I said.

"Then time's a wasting."

I didn't realize how right I was about "too long." Hadn't thought much about fences since Sarah left. No need with her horse gone, and I'd sold most of my cattle soon after.

As Charlie and I walked the fence, he took a verbal inventory. "Need new staples here. . . ." "Could stand a little tightening. . . ." "Post is gone — rotten at the ground. . . ." "New string of wire here."

"Tell you what," he said when we'd circled back to the barn, "I have a few more days before I need to deliver Snow White." He looked out across the pasture. "Why don't I help you get this fence in order?" He pushed his hands in his pockets and stepped back as though I needed room to think.

Maybe he couldn't read my mind, I thought, because the word "No" wasn't in there right now. Or maybe he knew I'd say "Yes" and just went through the formality of letting me decide. Then I thought — to hell with this mental exercise! "That'll be just fine," I said, "just fine."

Back into the shiny blue dually and off to the hardware store where we bought a bag of staples, a roll of barbed wire, and a half-dozen locust fence posts. Then Charlie drove me to Floyd's Feed and Seed to get the Blazer. Floyd was standing at the door. "How y'all making out?" He said "making out" several decibals louder than the rest.

I was about to yell, "None of your fucking business!" but Charlie answered first. "Just fine, Floyd, but we've got work to do."

We spent what was left of the afternoon until almost dark working on the fence. Charlie would catch wire in the claw of a hammer and pull the wire around the post so tight not even a skinny preacher could slip through the strands. Then I'd hold it in place while he nailed in new staples with another hammer. He kept checking on me. "Not too hard for you, Kate?" "Let me know if you get tired."

That old Robert Frost poem about mending fences kept running through my mind.

"Theirs was a stone wall," Charlie said, hammering a staple.

"Whose?"

"The neighbors in that Frost poem."

"What made you think of that?" "Don't know," he said not looking up. "And they were building a wall between them."

"What are we doing?" I asked.

"Mending fences," he said. He straightened his back and looked down the fence line like a surveyor pleased with what he saw. He stretched his arm out and took my hand. "And," he said, rubbing the back of my hand with his thumb, "we're working on the same side."

We walked toward the house carrying hammers, holding hands, and acting more like fifteen than fifty-something. When we reached the back porch, we flopped on the glider. "Kate McMahan," Charlie said, "know what you need?"

"A shower?" I said, pretending to pull away.

He pulled me back. "We both could use that. But something else?"

"A good meal?" I said.

"First part's right."

"A good . . ?" I knew where he was headed. But, hell, I didn't want to be too damn easy!

"A good man," he said, blowing out his chest.

"For what?" I asked, pushing his chest back in.

"A good man to," he said, pressing me down on the glider, belly first, "to rub your back!" With that he took those big hands, those big gentle hands and started squeezing the back of my neck and tops of my shoulders, then rubbing down my backbone between my shoulder blades all the way to the small of my back. Then up. Then down. Then across. Swaying the glider the whole time.

It felt so good. The touching. When you haven't been touched in a long time, you appreciate a good set of hands. Charlie seemed to enjoy it too. He would probably still be rubbing my back if I hadn't turned around. We didn't make kiss — not right away. We just held each other. Gliding and holding on, my face against his neck, my legs across his thighs. His arm curled around my back and his hand rested on my hip. He stroked the side of my face with his other hand. I felt like a little girl and a love-starved woman at the same time.

"Kate," he said. My name vibrated against my cheek. "It may sound silly," he hesitated, "but I think this is what's been pulling me."

"This?" I said, against his neck.

"You," he said, "being with you."

"On the glider?"

"And beyond." He traced my cheekbone with his fingers. "I want you. But I don't take making love lightly." He cleared his throat. "What about you?"

For the first time in my sexual life, I hesitated. I had taken it too lightly, much too lightly all these years. Here was this man I wanted to lie with, to touch, to kiss all over, to please — and all of a sudden I had an anxiety attack. What if I disappoint him? What if he doesn't like what he sees? I couldn't answer him.

Charlie sensed my uncertainty. "Maybe I'd better take a shower and cool off," he said. He set me to one side on the glider and stood up.

"Maybe so," I said. His lips smiled but his eyes didn't. "But," I added, "we're in the middle of a drought. And I need a shower too." For the first time since I'd known him, Charlie looked confused.

I sprung up from the glider, shook off my anxiety like dust, and hooked my arm in his. "We'd better shower together — to conserve water." He kissed me long and hard, then whispered in a voice deeper and hoarser than I'd heard before, "Lead the way."

That was Tuesday. Charlie stuck around all week. When we finished the fences, he found some loose shingles on the barn that needed nailing down. After that he replaced the hinges on the barn door. By Sunday he'd repaired enough, he said, to last at least a year. He decided he'd better head toward Georgia the next morning and deliver Snow White.

I really hated to see him load her into the trailer. I'd grown so accustomed to having her around, watching her delicate, graceful way of moving. That's what I told Charlie when he asked why I wasn't eating breakfast. "I'm going to miss Snow White," I said, not looking up.

"Oh," he said. Just "oh." For some reason that pissed me off. I started crying, crying like I haven't done since Vivienne died. I wanted to crawl up into the barn loft and scream myself out.

Charlie got up from the table and walked around behind my chair. He started squeezing and rubbing my shoulders like he did that first night. The more he rubbed, the harder I cried. "Come home with me, Kate," he said.

"I can't," I said, between sobs, "I can't leave here. It's all I have." God, I hated sounding like that, but I couldn't control the sudden pain in my heart.

He pulled me up from my chair and turned me toward him. I buried my face in his chest, but he caught the back of my hair and forced me to look up at him. "You can leave here if you love me," he said. "I'm more than a goddamn house and old memories!"

I got control of myself, enough to quit crying. He let me go and I walked with him out to his truck. "Goodbye, Charlie," I said. He didn't say anything. "Goodbye," I repeated. He still didn't answer. My throat knotted up and I couldn't say it again.

Finally, he said, "I'll be back in two day. That's two whole days to pack if you decide to come." He kissed me quickly and headed out. I stood there watching him go, wondering if I could ever say goodbye again.

That was a hour ago. I'm still sitting on the steps thinking about him when Donna's Honda rolls up the driveway. I look around to make sure there are no hoses in the way.

"Morning, Aunt Kate," she says, hopping out the car and pulling a basket of produce with her. "I'm giving this stuff away before Daddy comes over. Honestly, I can't freeze another pea or can another bean."

"You look tired," I say.

"Tired ain't the word for it." She dives in for another basket. "You'd think, with the drought and all, Daddy would slow down but he just gets another irrigation hose and lets it rip. They're saying don't water your lawns and gardens. Think I ought to turn Daddy in?"

I shake my head. "He'd disown you," I say.

"That's a thought," Donna says. I can't tell if she's kidding or not. "Well, I'm off. Got five more baskets to unload." With that she whips her Honda around and heads back out.

Before she clears the driveway, she has to pull over for a truck and trailer. It's blue and for just a second my heart leaps. But as it gets closer I see it's much older than Charlie's rig, much more dented too. Then I recognize it. And the driver. Mr. Living Color himself — Michael — riding up just like the hero in a Louis L'Amour novel.

I move from the steps to the shade of a big old elm tree near the driveway. He stops his truck in the shade. His window is already down. He's wearing a dark red shirt, Western style, with sleeves rolled up, resting in the window his tanned arm, almost golden. Goddamn it! I'm starting to sound like Sarah. Guess that's what a little romance can do to you.

"Hello, Michael," I say.

He sets his hat back a little, nods, and says, "Good morning, Kate." Then he adds, "How're things going?"

"What things?" I say. I don't plan to make this easy.

"The farm?"

"Still here," I answer, "hot and dry. But you can see that."

He looks around like he's noticing for the first time. "No hotter than the panhandle," he says, "but humid, a whole lot more humid." He wipes the back of his neck. "Where's that little red dog of yours?"

"Run over," I say, "more than a year ago." I let a minute or two pass. Then I ask, "What brings you this way?"

"The mare," Michael says, glancing a little too fast over his shoulder toward the trailer, "Sarah's mare. Thought I'd bring her back." I don't say anything but I'm wondering if "her" means the horse or Sarah. He gets out of the truck, looks into the trailer, then walks over to where I'm standing.

"Sarah still around?" he says almost casually but the word "Sarah" seems to stick in his throat.

"Yea," I say, "she's still around."

"How is she?" he says, glancing toward the barn.

"Fine," I say, "considering."

He looks me in the face. "Considering what?" he says.

"You know, her mother died."

"No, I didn't," he says, genuine surprise in his voice. "I knew she was sick, but I never heard any more."

Nor asked "any more," I'm thinking, but I don't say it. I hesitate a minute. "Then there's little Sammy," I say. Hell, I might as well get it out in the open.

"Little Sammy?"

"Sarah's baby." You'd think I plunged in a knife right at gut level. I watch this man of little emotion run through about a dozen. Finally he just stares at the ground. I stare at the same clump of dirt, starting to feel something, I'm not sure what, for him. Then he flattens the clump with his toe, looks me straight in the face, and says, "How old is he?"

"Who?" I say, my mind racing.

"Sarah's baby." He has me in an eye lock. Now I'm not afraid to tell anybody anything, but giving out the finer details of Sammy's birth is Sarah's decision. I'd already had my say on the matter.

"I'm not sure," I answer. "You'll have to ask his mother." I look him straight back into those dark brown eyes that must have driven Sarah crazy.

He looks away first. "I need to see her," he says, scanning the pasture like she might come riding up, "about the horse."

I volunteer to go after her. I know she won't come on her own and that it will be better all the way around if Michael avoids Jack.

"Why don't you unload Athene while I'm gone," I say, walking toward the house for my car keys. Michael looks relieved. His truck and trailer disappear around the far side of the barn as I head out.

On the drive to Sarah's, I consider what to tell her. As little as possible, I decide.

Sarah looks surprised but glad to see me. "Hi, Aunt Kate," she says. "Look who's here, Sammy." Sammy's in the middle of the kitchen floor, on his hands and knees, rocking back and forth like a hobby horse. "What brings you out on warm morning like this?" she asks.

I hesitate. "You need to come with me," I say, more solemn than I intend.

"Why?" Sarah asks, a note of panic in her voice. "Is it Jack?" I shake my head. "Donna? Daddy?" Her voice rises an octave with each name.

"No," I say, "everyone is fine. I just need your help." I'm starting to feel guilty. She calms down a little but still looks suspicious.

"I can't leave Sammy," she says.

"Bring him," I say, "he can help too." Judas, I think to myself. I feel like a goddamn Judas. But Sarah doesn't say anymore. She picks up Sammy, grabs an extra diaper and we're off. We don't talk much on the way to the farm. Sarah holds Sammy up to the window and they both look out as trees and buildings and telephone posts blur by. Doubts sail by in my mind like roadside signs. What if Michael breaks her heart again? What if he wants the baby? What if? What if?

"I think I'm doing the right thing," I blurt out loud.

"You are," another voice answers.

"What?" Sarah asks.

I look at her. "Nothing," I say. She turns toward the window again.

"You're doing the right thing," the voice repeats. This time I recognize it. Not Sarah's, not my own. The voice is Vivienne's.

[159

I park the Blazer in front of the barn. Sarah looks puzzled. "Let me hold Sammy," I say, easing him from her arms, "and come inside."

Sarah finds Athene. She lets out a cry and leaps for the mare's neck. She doesn't see Michael. Not yet. I can't stay any longer. It would be like watching a child have his appendix cut out. You know he'll be better off but you don't want to see the blood. "Here's Sammy," I say. She takes the baby, but her eyes are wild, so Harrison green, I wonder if I've made a mistake.

I give up little Samuel and head for the house. Once inside, I shout, "That's it, Vivienne, the last thing I can do for you."

SARAH

Have you ever awakened and felt like something was about to ignite or explode or fall to earth or fall away from earth? That's the way I feel this morning. Andrew would tell me it's anxiety brought on by "unsteady hormone levels induced by childbirth." Daddy would say it's "the pull of the moon." Donna would say "You got up on the wrong side of the mattress." Aunt Kate would call it "just a fucking awful morning." Jack wouldn't call it anything. I don't think the man has a moody bone in his body. At least not since Sammy was born.

Jack has his own style of handling the baby, somewhere between the Hope diamond and a basketball. He talks to him, changes his diaper, would breast-feed him if he could.

The day we came home from the hospital, Jack decided to introduce Sammy to Bilo. He crawled under the kitchen table on his hands and knees, actually on one hand, holding Sammy tight against his chest with the other hand. He squeezed in beside Bilo then carried on a conversation for both dog and baby. "Hi, Bilo," in a squeaky little voice, then "Arf! Baby!" in a barky voice, back and forth, so silly that I laughed until my sore abdomen ached.

He's still that way. The first time I had to go to Dr. Fleming for a recheck, Donna kept Sammy. But the next time Jack said, "I can take care of Sammy. No problem. And don't you call Donna Jean. She'll be over here all morning, talking nonstop." So I didn't. I left the two together assuming they both would be okay. I was half right.

When I came home, Jack was leaning over the crib, bobbing the upper half of his body, singing "Send in the Clowns." I slipped in beside him and looked down on Sammy. Sammy was fine. But Jack wasn't. He had this clown mobile Aunt Kate had given to Sammy suctioned to the center of his forehead. He swung around and nearly caught me in the face. A yellow clown and a red one twirled into an orange tangle.

Jack smiled, a little embarrassed-looking but mostly pleased with himself too. I could tell by the way he lifted his eyebrows and crinkled his forehead. Of course, it didn't crinkle evenly with the suction cup stuck in the center. "Sammy was crying so I thought I'd entertain him. See," Jack said, swinging back around and tangling three more clowns. "I just pulled it off the wall and stuck it to my forehead. It stayed on," he said tugging on the suction cup. "Really well," he added. It didn't budge. He pulled again, this time harder. I watched his skin stretch out from his forehead.

"It's stuck all right," I said. "Let me try." I wiggled it back and forth, then up and down. The clowns jigged in a spastic dance. Sammy waved his hands.

"You've got to break the seal," Jack said, his voice a note or two higher than usual. "Get a spoon."

I reached into the drawer, grabbed a spoon by the handle, and aimed for the suction cup glued to Jack's skin.

"For God's sake! Sarah!" Jack yelled, "that's a grapefruit spoon. I want you to break the seal not gouge out a chunk of my head like a grapefruit section!"

"Calm down," I told him, grabbing another spoon. I stuck the rounded tip right at the junction of skin and rubber, held onto the mobile, and pushed hard. The suction broke, clowns fell forward, Jack backward.

"Thank God!" he shouted, catching his balance. Then a little calmer, "thought I'd have to wear the damn thing to work." He rubbed his forehead.

"You'll have to wear 'part' of it," I said.

"What?"

"Look in the mirror."

"Jesus," Jack said. In the center of his forehead was the biggest, brightest, roundest hicky I've ever seen.

[161

We tried combing his hair forward — too short. Band-Aids — took too many. Revlon cover stick — he said he couldn't live with himself if he used makeup. Finally, he concocted a story about tripping over a lamp cord and falling head first onto a door knob. Then he made me swear on the sanctity of motherhood not to tell anyone, especially Donna.

He checked on Sammy again, grabbed some sunglasses, kissed me, and headed out to work singing "Send in the Clowns" more like Janis Joplin than Judy Collins. I sat in the middle of the nursery floor, untangling clowns and wondering how I could have ever left this man.

Thinking about Jack's hickey doesn't even get me out of this blue mood today. Maybe I'm worried about Donna. Jack says she's just getting older "like the rest of us." Aunt Kate thinks, whatever the reason, it's an improvement because Donna doesn't echo Andrew like she used to. Wonder how Andrew analyzes the situation — that is if he's noticed? I'm not sure Donna even knows what it is. I do. Restlessness — plain and simple. But there's no "plain and simple" way to deal with it. That's what worries me.

Donna stopped by one day last week. She was wearing her usual hot weather clothes — camp shirt, Bermuda shorts, tennis shoes — but her face looked different. She jumped out of her Honda and ran to the door, acting happier than I'd seen her in weeks. I hadn't really talked with her in weeks either. But Sammy was napping and I was glad for her visit.

"Notice anything different?" she asked, blinking her eyelids.

"New shoes?"

She checked her feet. "No." She lifted her hands to her face and patted her cheeks.

"New dress?" I said.

"No-o-o, Sarah!" She blinked a few more times and patted her cheeks harder.

"I get it!" I said, shielding my eyes. "It's your radiant beauty! You've been MADE-OVER!"

"Bingo!" she said, bending her knees into a curtsy. "Holly's cousin did it just now in Holly's shop. Can you really tell a difference?"

I nodded.

"I started to have it done gradual like those men who turn their hair back a little at a time with Grecian Formula. Base and blush one week. Lipliner and lipstick the next. Eye shadow, eyeliner, mascara and on and on. But then I thought, why not go whole hog and do it all at once."

"You look great," I said. "How much was it?"

Donna cleared her throat. "$76," she whispered, "with starter kit and all. So, honestly, what do you think?"

"Worth every penny," I said. "Has Andrew seen you?"

She shook her head. "I'm not going to tell him, unless he notices on his own, or Daddy or the twins either." She stared beyond me. Her face clouded.

"Your eyes look so blue," I said, wanting her good mood to continue, "bluer than I've ever seen them."

"They're blue all right," she said. Then she looked back at me. "Holly's cousin Barb used this highlighter she called brick powder or powder brick — meaning the color, not ground up brick or anything. She said it magnifies whatever color your eyes already are." She smiled and blinked again.

"What about your hair?" I asked.

"What about it?" Her smile uncurled. "Does it need changing too?"

"Oh, no," I said, wishing I hadn't mentioned hair. "It always looks nice, curly and nice."

"Truth is," Donna said, sounding somewhat pacified, "I thought about giving up perms and getting one of those short blow-dry jobs." She swept her hair up and away from her face. "What do you think?"

"Oh, Nonna! You'd be pretty bald." I threw my arms around her.

She hugged me back. A desperate hug. "You haven't called me 'Nonna' since you left. I've missed you so much!" she said. Then she began to cry.

"What's wrong?" I asked.

"Nothing," she sobbed.

"Nothing?"

"Everything!"

"Like what?" I asked. But she shook her head between sobs. I held her until she was cried out. Then Sammy woke up. Donna went into the bathroom, repaired her make-over as best she could, and left. After she was gone, it hit me. Donna wasn't crying just about her hair or even about missing me. There was sadness much deeper and stronger. And her crying wasn't soft and dainty whimpers like it used to be. It was painful, jagged, ugly sobs like mine always was.

Donna's acting more and more like Mama — busy, fidgety, distracted at times. Mama. She was buried a year ago today. No wonder I feel so unsettled. If only Mama could see Sammy. She'd love him just like Daddy. And she'd forgive me, too, like Daddy has. He hasn't said so but I can see it in his eyes. I understand now what came between us for so long, even before the first time I tried to run away.

He's back to gardening. Donna said he let his plot go to weed last year when Mama was sick. Probably the only time in his life that he wasn't growing something. Daddy always said gardening was nature's way of training humans. Sometimes he does what he calls "garden experiments." Like with his mantelpiece cucumber. Donna and I called it his riddle pickle. One summer when we were still kids, Daddy tried an experiment in his cucumber patch. He took an empty vinegar bottle and slipped a blossom, still on the vine, through the small glass neck. Then he pushed the bottle under the plant. He asked Donna and me if we thought it could grow. We both said no, not without soil or light. But in a few weeks Daddy led us back to the same patch in his garden, like the maître d' in a fine restaurant, and showed us the bottle. There inside was a huge white cucumber. He said it didn't turn green like the other cucumbers because it didn't get enough light, but it still grew because the vine nourished it. He broke off the vine, filled the bottle with vinegar, screwed on the lid, and set his masterpiece of an experiment on the living room mantel next to Mama's Royal Dalton dancing girl. "A reminder," he said, "of the wonders of nature."

Daddy's growing another one this year to commemorate Sammy's birth. Jack says a savings bond would be more practical. He and Daddy don't get along as well as they once did. They compete for Sammy. Andrew says it's the "first-son versus the first-grandson syndrome." I know he made that up, but it fits. Donna says getting Sammy away from Daddy is harder than "sweeping slugs off of concrete." That fits too.

Aunt Kate sits back and laughs at both Jack and Daddy, more than she should I think. But it's good to see her happy again. Her first new boyfriend in two years, according to Donna. She says he hasn't done a single "inside" repair or addition to the house but he and Aunt Kate have spent a lot of time outdoors. That's good to hear. I know she loves that old farm house but I think it has too many ghosts for her. Donna thinks Aunt Kate might even consider leaving with this llama guy. I can't imagine her giving up the farm and going all the way to Washington. But she may. If I've learned one thing in the past two years, it's that you can't predict what people will do based on what they've done in past, especially your own self.

I'm standing at the kitchen sink, staring out the window and thinking about Aunt Kate when I see her blue Blazer ease up the driveway. She doesn't see me from the window. She looks upset. My anxiety reaches flood stage.

"Hi, Aunt Kate," I say, opening the door, my voice unsteady. She doesn't make a move to come inside, doesn't say anything for a moment. My mind whirls — visions of Jack holding his chest, Daddy facedown in his garden, Donna in a crumpled Honda.

Aunt Kate looks at Sammy. She finally speaks. "You need to come with me," she says. Then, as though she knows what I'm thinking, she adds, "Everyone's fine. I just need your help." I can tell by the way she sets her jaw, she's not going to explain.

"Jack won't be home till lunch time. I don't have anybody to keep Sammy," I say.

"Bring him."

We ride the five miles to her farm almost in silence. I stare out the window, try to empty myself from anxiety by absorbing the scenery. From the crunch of my driveway and out my street, onto the four-lane then back off, around the curve at Cater's Bridge, past the Short Stop Bar and Grill, past Pilgrim's Dairy, then up the bumpy dirt road to the farm.

Aunt Kate drives straight to the barn then stops. She turns and looks at me. I can see a range of emotions in her eyes — sadness, love, resolution. Now she'll tell me, I think to myself, why she wanted me to come. Instead, she takes Sammy and says, "Follow me."

She leads me into the barn and towards the back stall. It's dark, almost dark as night. The air is charged. I feel it popping against my skin, inside my head. My heart beats faster with each step. I can barely catch my breath. Aunt Kate stops. "There," she says, gesturing with her head. "Look in there."

The stall is half obscured in darkness. Out of the shadow, like a flashback or a dream, steps Athene, my beautiful roan mare. I slip through the stall door, throw myself against her, rub her neck, run my hand down her leg, tug on her mane, and breathe in that wonderful horse scent — sensations I haven't felt for an entire year. It seems now for a lifetime.

I turn to Aunt Kate. "How . . ? Where . . ?"

"Ask him," she says, looking beyond Athene. She hands me Sammy and walks away. I turn back to the mare, see movement in the darkness.

"Hello, Sarah." I am paralyzed by the voice — unable to speak, move, think — able only to search the dark for the speaker, for Michael. He moves out of the shadow to the other side of the mare, stretches his arm around her neck, close enough now that I can see his face.

"Couldn't sell her," he says. His voice sounds strained. "Didn't seem right, her being yours and all. And I thought," he clears his throat, "I thought you might be back for her." I say nothing. "Can hardly see my hand in front of my face in here," he says. "Let's go outside." He opens the stall door. My legs feel weak but they carry me toward the light.

Outside, my eyes drink him in — beard thicker than I remember, worn denim, arms shining golden in the sun. He looks at Sammy. Then he turns his dark eyes on me. I fall in.

"See you've been busy," he says with a laugh that isn't really a laugh. "When did he come along?"

"What?" I hear myself say, trying to stop my descent into his eyes.

"When was he born?" Michael says. His eyes have me tumbling.

"This spring," the words break out of my throat. "Came a little early."

"Spring or the baby?" His eyes shift from me to Sammy then back to me.

I feel my balance returning. "Both," I say. "I was born a little early too."

"Must run in the family," he says. He reaches for Sammy. I reluctantly give him up. Michael holds him at arm's length, studies

166]

his face. "Where'd he get these eyes?" he asks. "Does that run in your family too?"

"No," I say. "I don't think so."

Michael smiles. Then pulls Sammy in close. "I've seen eyes like these before." He rubs his hand gently over the crest of Sammy's head.

"You have?"

"It's fairly common in some breeds of dogs — huskies, setters — occasionally a horse will have different-colored eyes. But you see it in people too." He doubles his arms underneath Sammy like a hammock and sways his shoulders back and forth.

"I haven't," I say.

"I have," he says, more to Sammy than me. Then he turns his eyes on me again. "It tends to be hereditary."

"Must come from Jack's side," I say, not blinking. "How's Texas?"

"Still there when I left it."

"How about Pete and Norris?"

"Same," he said. "Pete's still nailing shoes and Norris is still running horses in circles." He stops swinging Sammy and cradles him in his left arm. "Back in the spring, just at dusk one day, Pete and I found a rattlesnake stretched out near the fence. We tried to scare it off before the horses caught its scent. I swear, Sarah, it was as big around as my arm." He holds out his right arm for measure, one of those hard, tanned forearms that electrified me more than two years ago. I feel the current again. I try not to show it.

"Damn thing wrapped itself around a post and hissed and hissed until the horses went wild. They were running around the pen, bumping into each other, trying to break down the fence." He shifts Sammy to his right arm. "We had to take a shovel and kill it," he says, sorrow in his voice. "I'd rather have shot the thing and gotten it over with. But that would have make the horses crazier."

"It might have bitten you or Pete or one of the ranch hands," I say.

"Maybe so," he says, "but it doesn't seem right to kill something because you're afraid of it."

He looks out across the pasture toward the mountain range. "I missed the mountains," he says.

"Hard to see them this late in the summer," I say. "The air's too thick. Takes a cool fall day to bring them out again."

"From here it does," he says, "but not in Tennessee. They're all around you." He looks at me again. "That's where I am now. Have been for the past two months."

"In Tennessee?" I ask, my voice too high.

He nods. "Been staying with Russell and Annie. Remember them?"

"Of course," I say, my mind back in the coolness of their home.

"I bought some land nearby — room enough for a cabin, a small barn, little bit of pasture. A small stream runs along the lower edge. It's really pretty. You'd love it." I can't think of anything to say but he seems wound up. "Plenty of horses in the nearest town, a few trail-ride outfits, and a stable or two. Enough to keep me busy."

"Guess they can always use a traveling vet," I say.

He doesn't seem to hear me. "The other morning before sunset, I walked out to my little piece of mountain. I wanted to watch the sun rise so I could decide exactly where to mark the foundations for the cabin, the right slant so I can watch the sun come up every morning if I want to. As the sun rose through the pines, mist from the creek lifted. It turned pink, this whole line of pink fog rising through the green pines. Really beautiful." He looks into my eye and says, "It made me think of you." I feel his hand slipping around my heart, tightening.

"Then I walked down to the creek. There stood a doe and her fawn looking back at me. For a minute they just stood there, dreamlike with the mist rising around them." Sammy starts to squirm. Michael shifts him to his other side. "Can you imagine such a view from your own back porch?"

I shake my head and look at Sammy. My arms feel empty.

"There's a big old oak tree right where I want the cabin. I'm going to cut it down when I get back and take it to the sawmill. Russell says there's one about twenty miles away. He's offered to help me build some furniture out of the lumber — a slab table and benches, some other pieces. But the first thing I want make to is a platform bed. Remember the one we . . . the one at Russell's? That's what I'm going to build first. What do you think?" He watches me. I don't answer. I reach for Sammy. Fill my arms with him.

Michael stands there, hands on his hips, looking better than anything Zane Gray or Barbara Cartland could come up with, better than any mythical hero my own mind could create. I don't want to

168]

give him up. I feel that familiar stir of restlessness. Sammy seems to feel it too. He wiggles in my arms.

"I'm using the plans we drew up for the cabin," Michael says. "Remember the plans?" I nod. "There'll be plenty of room."

"For what?" I ask.

"For you," he says, "and the baby," he pauses, "if you want to come along."

"If you want to come along" rings in my ears. Not "I love you" or "I need you" or "I'm claiming you and my son" but "if you want to come along." Standing there, staring at Michael I realize what attracted me beyond pure lust. Michael is the kind of man who is content on his own. His love of nature, horses, freedom to move on when he gets restless or crowded is enough for him. He may stay in Tennessee for a while, but sooner or later, he'll move on. The year we spent together, our restlessness wasn't the same. He was looking to see and I was looking to find. I need connections.

I have Sammy — and Jack who would probably fight to the death for this child he claims as his own. I can't leave him again. It will kill what I love most about him — his confident, innocent way of figuring solutions to whatever problems life gives him.

Then there's Daddy to consider. I don't think he can take another loss. Donna needs me too. She's about ready to make a break herself. And if Andrew hasn't sensed it yet, I may have to draw him a diagram, complete with a lecture on restless Crawford women.

"I'll think about you and the cabin and Tennessee," I say, "but Sammy and I'd better stick around here."

He shifts his hat forward. I can barely see his eyes. "I understand," he says. If he's disappointed, he doesn't show it. He may even be relieved a little. "I'll keep an eye out for a pony just right for Sammy," he says. "Next time I'm down this way, I'll bring it by."

He gets into his old pickup and heads down Aunt Kate's driveway. I wave but he doesn't look back. I watch him until the last tip of the horse trailer disappears. I glance toward the sun. Almost straight up.

"Must be about noon," I say to Sammy. I retrieve a diaper from Aunt Kate's car and walk toward the house.

Aunt Kate sits on the screen porch gliding back and forth, back and forth like a sign in the wind. She watches us. I slip through the screen door. She stops the glider while Sammy and I settle

[169

beside her. Then she presses with her toe and sets the glider swaying again. The motion is soothing, like a swing or a rocking chair or a mother's arms. We glide in silence several minutes.

Aunt Kate speaks first. "Is he gone?" she asks, not breaking our rhythm.

"Yes," I answer on the forward swing, "he's gone." Backward swing, "Michael is gone." I feel like I'm chanting a nursery rhyme or a fairy tale. Sammy nuzzles my neck.

"For good?" Aunt Kate asks, not looking at me.

"I suppose," I say, "if there are any good departures."

"There are some," she says. A complete swing. Another one. She looks into my eyes and stops the glider. "Ready to go home?"

"Yes," I say, looking back into her eyes and feeling more certain than I have about anything in two whole years, maybe a lifetime. Sammy wiggles. "But," I add, "I'd better change his diaper first."

I head for Aunt Kate's bedroom. Her bed is filled with suitcases and piles of clothes. I wedge Sammy between two piles. Aunt Kate didn't mention a trip, I think as I change Sammy. Beside one suitcase lies the portrait of Mama and Aunt Kate as girls, the little one she always kept in the desk drawer. Suddenly my heart begins pounding all the way to my head. My throat feels tight as a scar. I lift Sammy and walk slowly back to the porch. Aunt Kate is gliding back and forth again.

"Going somewhere?" I ask, my voice thin enough to crack.

She nods.

"Where?"

"Washington," she says, gliding forward.

"To see Charlie?"

Back and forth, back and forth. "With Charlie," she answers. "With" echoes inside my head.

"A week or two?" I can't hold back the sound of desperation.

She plants both feet and stops the glider. "Maybe for good."

"But, Aunt Kate, what about the farm?"

"Joe can take care of it."

"Daddy can't take care of himself," I say. "He depends on Donna for everything."

"It'll be good for him. Get him out of Donna's hair." She leans forward, arches her back. "Besides, he always wanted to live out here. Got mad when Papa left the farm to me." She stands up. "I'll be back from time to time to check on things."

"You'll be back?" I ask, hanging onto her words.

"For a visit," she says.

I want to scream, "You can't leave! You can't!" But I fight for control, breathe deep, so deep that Sammy struggles in my tight arms. "What if things with Charlie don't work out?" I say, more rational than I feel.

"It's time I took a chance," Aunt Kate says. She slips her arm around me. "You, of all people, should understand that."

I nod. "But what will I do without you?" I'm crying now.

Aunt Kate takes Sammy. Looks into his round, smooth face. "Life keeps changing, Sarah. You can't slow it down and you can't back it up."

I look into her eyes and I see happiness, like the girl in the portrait with Mama. I wipe my own eyes, kiss Aunt Kate's cheek, and slip Sammy from her arms. "How about giving us a lift home?" I say, "Jack will be waiting."